MW01256810

Putin's Mafia State:

How Russia Failed to Become a Democracy

EDITED BY

LEONID NEVZLIN

Producer & International Distributor
eBookPro Publishing
www.ebook-pro.com

PUTIN'S MAFIA STATE: HOW RUSSIA FAILED TO BECOME A DEMOCRACY

EDITED BY LEONID NEVZLIN

ISBN 9789655754148

Contents

Foreword

This book was co-authored by several people, some of whom still live in Russia. Therefore, I cannot name them, for fear they will be persecuted and jailed. I edited this book, and I am grateful to the authors who bravely worked on it for the last two years. I am grateful to everyone who helped prepare and write this book.

I have had no ties of any kind to Russia for a long time; I have been living in Israel for over 20 years, I am an Israeli citizen, publisher, and public figure. I believe it is very important, especially now, to fight the mafia and terror in any shape and form they may take. Russia is a key link in the chain of forces that want to destroy and annihilate the world founded on democratic values as they perceive this world as a threat to their personal power and wealth.

Why is this book important to the Western reader? It provides a better understanding of what has been happening in Russia over the last 20 years, why Russia veered off the path toward democracy, eventually not only invading and terrorizing a neighboring country but also becoming a threat to the world community and Russian citizens alike. Politicians in the democratic world must realize why it is impossible and even dangerous to attempt Realpolitik relations or try to achieve compromises and find mutual interests with a mafia state.

I am not talking just about Russia. Any country can run the risk of a mafia regime taking over. This is why it is so important to understand the nature of a mafia regime and identify its hallmarks. A civil society thus has time to prevent a nation from becoming a mafia state.

Leonid Nevzlin

Introduction

The war against Ukraine unleashed by Vladimir Putin was a logical act of the political regime that has formed in Russia. This regime cannot be characterized as a run-of-the mill authoritarianism or dictatorship. The most accurate definition of such a regime was formulated by the Hungarian political scientist Bálint Magyar,[1] who called this type of government a "mafia state." After a year and a half of active fighting, a series of events in Russia and abroad have obliterated any remaining doubts that Russia today is a typical example of a mafia state.

On August 23, 2023, a plane crashed in Russia's Tver Region, which killed the top management of the Wagner private security company, including its founder Evgeny Prigozhin. This happened exactly two months after

---

1 B. Magyar "Anatomiya postkommunisticheskikh mafioznikh gosudarstv" [English version: A Concise Field Guide to Post-Communist Regimes: Actors, Institutions, and Dynamics (from Amazon), https://www.amazon.com/Concise-Field-Guide-Post-Communist-Regimes/dp/9633865875/ref=pd_bxgy_img_sccl_1/139-9621826-1861217?pd_rd_w=4GeH7&content-id=amzn1.sym.26a5c67f-1a30-486b-bb90-b523ad38d5a0&pf_rd_p=26a5c67f-1a30-486b-bb90-b523ad38d5a0&pf_rd_r=8SH5MME2WXTP4YEMGQQG&pd_rd_wg=qFz2w&pd_rd_r=451f537d-e1ea-4ea9-bbb4-1a53a44c3b72&pd_rd_i=9633865875&psc=1]. References are to the Russian edition.

Prigozhin's attempted revolt and the Wagner "march on Moscow." At the time, Vladimir Putin described it as a "betrayal." The plane crash became the catalyst that impelled experts at various levels to assert that Russia operates according to mafia rules. The plane crash, indeed, makes perfect sense if you apply the criteria and hallmarks of a mafia state.

Actually, the nature of the regime that has formed in Russia became clear much earlier. Boris Nemtsov declared that "Putin's Russia is a mafia state."2 Garry Kasparov talked and wrote about it on numerous occasions, noting: "What has emerged in Russia is not a classic dictatorship, but a mafia state," and Mikhail Khodorkovsky warned that "Putin is a mob boss running the Russian government like a criminal syndicate."[3]

Western politicians realized it, too. French President Emmanuel Macron noted in February 2023: "I talked to Putin a year ago, and he assured me that Russia has nothing in common with the Wagner group. I accepted that. Today, we see that the Wagner group is involved in the war against Ukraine. This means that Russia is an ordinary mafia state." U.S. Secretary of State Antony Blinken said that, after his campaign against Moscow, Prigozhin should be concerned about his safety and saving his own life. After Prigozhin's plane crashed, U.S.

---

2 https://inosmi.ru/20110404/168063342.html [Russian].

3 https://www.bild.de/bild-plus/politik/ausland/politik-ausland/chodorkowski-ueber-putin-russland-funktioniert-wie-eine-mafia-62394092,jsRedirectFrom=conversionToLogin,view=conversionToLogin.bild.html [German].

President Joe Biden said he wasn't surprised to hear the news. This means that U.S. politicians have an excellent understanding of exactly what type of regime is in place in Russia.

This book's authors seek to describe Russia's political system in detail, to analyze its driving mechanisms, and understand what sustains it. We will closely examine the concept of a "mafia state" and discuss how Russia became such a state, and describe its characteristics and how it functions.

WHY PRECISELY A "MAFIA STATE"?

For starters, let's clarify why we say "mafia state." In modern political science, there are many other definitions to describe political regimes that fall outside the traditional spectrum spanning "authoritarianism" to "democracy." Regimes with features of both authoritarianism and democracy are most often described as falling into a gray area, or as *hybrid* regimes. Such regimes are not democratic in nature, although they appear similar to democracies and possess certain features of democracies – such as elections, separation of powers, and so forth. In such regimes, however, democratic institutions are merely for show; they are make-believe, while the regime itself is more authoritarian. One type of such a regime is *electoral authoritarianism*. This term means that such political systems have the institution of elections, but elections are for show only and do not serve to ensure a regime changeover, nor do they ensure representation of various political forces.

If we go outside the "authoritarianism – democracy" spectrum, we may encounter a whole range of definitions for the regime that has formed in Russia. For example, we often see the word "*kleptocracy*." The term "kleptocrat" was first introduced in 1968 by Stanislav Andreski to describe a head of state or high-ranking official who seeks mainly to enrich himself and has sufficient power to do so using his official position. This definition most closely fits what was happening in Russia until 2022, although it fails to take into account a number of singularities.

A kleptocracy chiefly utilizes a situation for its own benefit without changing the form of government. Income is redirected using classical corruption mechanisms without radically changing the sources of income. A kleptocracy does not necessarily use either political or economic violence. Forcible appropriation of property under such regimes is rather rare, and kleptocrats do not create stable vassal ties or relationships of subordination. As a rule, a kleptocracy has no international ambitions or operations.

A kleptocracy can be viewed as a more extreme case of a corrupt regime, but a corrupt or oligarchic regime does not enable a political force to obtain essentially a limitless monopoly on power, limitless freedom to change the Constitution and appoint its own people to all key positions in the state. In corrupt or oligarchic systems, competition among various groups of influence in the country is maintained; there is no total seizure of power.

One also encounters the term "*silovarchy*," to characterize the Russian regime; *it accentuates the predominance of security and intelligence agents in politics and the economy.*[4] For example, South Korea and Indonesia were *silovarch* states. At one point, Russia was categorized as

---

4 Daniel Treisman, *Putin's Silovarchs*, 2006. https://www.sscnet.ucla.edu/polisci/faculty/treisman/Papers/siloct06.pdf

a *silovarchy* because Putin and some of his entourage came from security and intelligence agencies. It's true that former and acting *siloviki*, Putin's colleagues from the KGB and FSB [post-Soviet term for the state security agency], have significant influence in Russia. If we take a look, however, at the entire spectrum of the regime's beneficiaries, those who influence monetary flows, those who hold real – not nominal – power in the country, then we see that *siloviki* are just one structural link.

Another researcher, the Swedish economist and specialist on the East European economy, Anders Åslund, called the Russian political system "*crony capitalism.*"[5] This term highlights access to income, and, to a lesser extent, notes the ability to use tools of violence, both legal and illegal ones. This term became less relevant, however, after military action in Ukraine.

Intimidation for political goals, utilizing state resources to obtain an advantage in business or otherwise, concealing wealth by using fronts, formation of a structurally organized group that replaced official government bodies, striving for a monopoly on power – all this is typical of the mafia as an organization, and typical of a mafia state when it encompasses the entire system of governance. This is exactly what has happened in Russia since 2000, which is why we believe the term "mafia state" most accurately describes the system that has formed in Russia under Vladimir Putin.

---

5 Anders Åslund, *Russia's Crony Capitalism: The Path from Market Economy to Kleptocracy.* (New Haven: Yale University Press, 2019).

What is a mafia state?

It is incorrect to understand "mafia state" as referring to a nation where power is held by criminals and the mafia. This would be a too narrow interpretation. We will instead use the concept developed by the Hungarian sociologist and politician Bálint Magyar, who published his book *Post-Communist Mafia State: The Case of Hungary*.[6] Two authors – Bálint Madlovics and Bálint Magyar published an open access sequel in 2020 entitled *The Anatomy of Post-Communist Regimes – a Conceptual Framework*.[7]

In his book, Magyar described the basic characteristics of a mafia state and how such regimes operate. He defines post-communist mafia states as an independent subset of autocracy, a form of *criminal state*.

In a mafia state, governance goals are *amassing political power while increasing the mafia's wealth through state means*. This is accomplished by using a monopoly

---

6 Bálint Magyar, *Post-Communist Mafia State: The Case of Hungary* (Budapest: Central European University Press, 2016). The book was published in Russian translation three years later.

7 Bálint Magyar, Bálint Madlovics, *Post-communist regimes. A Conceptual Structure.* — Novoye Literaturnoe Obozrenie. This citation is from a Russian-language publication. In English the book is titled *The Anatomy of Post-Communist Regimes – a Conceptual Framework* [English title from https://ceupress.com/book/anatomy-post-communist-regimes].

on violence in an atmosphere of mafia culture elevated to state policy. To put it simply, in a mafia state, a small group of people who possess power use the state and its resources for personal enrichment and to maintain uninterrupted power. These actions are beyond the reach of justice; they are supported by security and intelligence agencies and concealed by the din of the state propaganda machine.

In other words, in a mafia state, the ruling group's goals have little to do with society's well-being – instead, these goals are fully in line with Italy's Criminal Code definition of the mafia.8 Enrichment mostly occurs through access to authority and state funds, through government contracts and top positions in state companies. This is why the main goal becomes staying in power, which ensures the continuity of this process and eliminates risks both in the present and in the future.

---

8 In 1982, the Italian Criminal Code introduced Article 416-bis, which gives a legal definition of the mafia: "*A Mafia-type organization is an organization whose members use the power of intimidation deriving from the bonds of membership, the state of subjugation and conspiracy of silence that it engenders to commit offences, to acquire direct or indirect control of economic activities, licences, authorizations, public procurement contracts and services or to obtain unjust profits or advantages for themselves or others, or to prevent or obstruct the free exercise of vote, or to procure votes for themselves or others at elections.*" [English taken from chrome-extension://efaidnbmnnnibpcajpcglclefindmkaj/https://www.legal-tools.org/doc/b8efae/pdf/#:~:text=Persons%20belonging%20to%20a%20Mafia,years%20for%20that%20offence%20alone].

The government apparatus becomes a tool for achieving mafia objectives and serves to protect the regime that has formed – the mafia system. Thus, the group of *mafiosi* has full access to all the tools for distributing benefits, controlling resources, and using coercion in the name of the state. Anyone trying to fight the mafia structure that has penetrated into and absorbed the government is declared an "extremist."

An informal group of people, a crime syndicate that constantly must impart legitimacy to its volition constitutes the ruling core of the mafia state. *It imposes its will using pseudo-democratic institutions, the parliament, the government, and the mafia state-controlled media.* These purportedly *"democratic" institutions do not work to coordinate various interests – they camouflage the essence of the mafia state, and become subservient to it.*

According to Bálint Magyar, a main principle of the mafia state is that *private interests replace societal interests, and not just once in a while, but constantly and systematically.* Essentially all spheres of state activity are subordinate to the mafia clan's interests of reinforcing their power and clan enrichment. The mafia's actions of amassing political power and enriching itself always go hand-in-hand; they are interdependent, and they are both the goal and the means to achieve it. State policy goals are secondary in matters of making political decisions. Magyar says that any and all decisions involve both power and property simultaneously.

The head of a mafia state does not govern a country – he unlawfully runs it as if he owns it. On paper, the country has all the requisite institutions – a president, a parliament, a government. But in reality, power is held by a group of people joined by close, often familial ties, and the president represents specifically that group. That group is a hierarchy; it is impossible for an outsider to join the group, and it is equally impossible for a group member voluntarily to leave.

In a mafia state, decisions are made outside official, legitimate organizations: instead, a small mafia circle is the ultimate – albeit informal and illegitimate – decision-maker. Low-level decisions are often also made informally by an individual instead of a formal authority. Many rulings can be bought and sold. One of the most popular services is criminal law: for a fee, one can have a criminal case opened or closed. Even official positions at the municipal or state level are sometimes bought and sold, becoming a link in the money-power-money trade chain.

What are the hallmarks of a mafia state?

1. Hallmarks of a mafia state: clan structure

A mafia state's clans develop from a small circle of the clan leader's *confidants.*

Loyalty and faithfulness to the clan and its leader are the main clan membership requirements. In a mafia state, aside from constant enrichment, the clan is primarily focused on keeping the clan in power as long as possible. This is why the country's entire political system is restructured – in order to *guarantee keeping the ruling group in power as long as possible.* This allows the group to keep the loot, prevent an investigation into the legality of the group's enrichment, and guarantee an uninterrupted income. All political institutions – especially legislative and judicial – serve the mafia state, which also controls elections, the media, and nonprofit organizations.

Mafia state members most often enrich themselves secretly using *fronts*, registering mafia members' property in the names of relatives, bodyguards, service staff or confidants largely unknown to the public at large. The role of these front men is great.

The mafia circle consists of insiders and yes-men who play by the given rules, no matter how illegal. Everyone in the group becomes bound by power, property, illegal activity, and collective responsibility. A yes-man doesn't ask too many questions, and he works within the system in accordance with its rules.

A mafia clan is most often built on close informal ties – those of family, friendship, or profession. These ties are both a prerequisite and a guarantee of loyalty.

2. Hallmarks of a mafia state: misappropriation of state property

In a mafia state, mafia resources and state resources are one and the same. Magyar notes: "*The mafia's property and public, or state property, are invariably intermixed.*" The head of state runs the country as if it were his private estate. A powerful mafia group takes over the main state resources and allocates state income as it sees fit. No outsiders are allowed into this circle.

In a mafia state, the economic structure changes: competition is eliminated, while entire industries (primarily the most profitable ones) are monopolized in the mafia group's interests. Assets are reallocated to benefit either the state or the businessmen who are part of, or loyal to, the mafia group.

Magyar describes these mafia state processes as follows: Attempts are made to misappropriate successful enterprises that are not linked to the mafia family, sometimes using violence or state resources. A mafia state redistributes property through legalized robbery, taking property arbitrarily, without a legal basis. They take what pleases them, asserts Magyar. In a mafia state, an independent business (if it still exists), is forced to look for ways *to protect itself from a government takeover.*

In a mafia state, property ownership is conditional: it is given and taken away at the clan leader's will. Property ownership is unstable; the right to ownership and the expansion of such ownership depend on how loyal one is to the clan.

The mafia state is predatory. The booty, the loot gained through special operations (most often conducted in the name of the state) become the clan's property. Most domestic economic booty is gained using hostile takeovers with the help of the state's security and intelligence services. Abroad, it is secured through wars of aggression or by using the resources of dependent territories.

3. Hallmarks of a mafia state: informal ties and unwritten rules

Order in a mafia state is not based on laws: it is based on personal ties and informal agreements. In such a state, "protectors" and "negotiators" play an important role. "Protectors" ensure security, property ownership and status behind the scenes, while "negotiators" build ties, solve problems, coordinate interests, and enable unofficial money flows.

Money is often the key to solving a problem or coordinating interests (such as splitting the turf or dividing resources). Money is the main "lubricant" for all processes, and without money, nothing works in a mafia state. This is why, *in a mafia state, corruption is no longer something extraordinary – it becomes systemic and integral.* Without corruption (monetary lubricant), a rusty mafia state machine cannot operate. Processes grind to a halt until the system is re-lubricated. A mafia state is virtually devoid of idealists or selfless people; the understanding is that someone always gets their cut, and others' interests must always be considered. Access to power, resources, and connections becomes the source of income and wealth. Power and money are indivisibly intertwined.

In a mafia state, the "*front man*" emerges – an on-paper property owner or decision maker. The front man's only requirements are loyalty and silence. If something goes wrong, the front man can be done away with, and precisely for that reason, in a mafia state such people sometimes die unexpectedly or under suspicious circumstances.

In order for the system to function properly, a "curator" is often assigned in order to make sure that the mafia clan's will is executed at the lower levels. The "curator" *does not merely supervise, he also "interprets" the language of law into the language of mob rules.* The "curator" often acts as a "negotiator" or knows to whom to turn for problem resolution in a crisis situation. Any problem becomes solvable, any problem can be handled, even if not quite legally. In a mafia state, any law can be circumvented if needed or rewritten to suit the mob.

Laws don't work as they do in a healthy society: instead, mob rules and unwritten rules apply. A mafia state does not uphold the law. It breaks the law at will and monopolizes the ability to change laws to benefit the ruling group. Only "insiders" can break the law, and they do so in the clan's interests.

Criminality is either permissible or forbidden. A crime is not punishable unless the perpetrator falls out of favor with the clan – e.g., breaks unspoken agreements and mob rules (for example, fails to give someone their cut, gets greedy, stands in the way of group insiders making money, or uses the security or media structures against another clan member).

In a mafia state, the most serious issues are coordinated with the head of the mafia state, who plays the role of an arbiter, a "fixer." In order to start any project (especially one that's not quite legal or one that impinges upon another clan member's interests) or to have someone appointed to a certain post, the boss has to give the green light. This nod of approval ensures that no problems arise. Failure to inform the clan leader of an upcoming project is a serious transgression.

4. Hallmarks of a mafia state: fake institutions

A mafia state builds Potemkin villages instead of real government institutions. In a mafia state, other entities replace official institutions of power. Traditional institutions merely pretend to continue functioning. They exist, but they lack influence, they are merely for show. The mafia state uses these institutions to put on a show when needed – in order to make it appear that democracy, rule of law, society, diversity, etc., are really in place. All institutions are hollowed out and become empty shells, called upon to support mafia politics at the right time. Real power moves to totally different, informal structures not described anywhere, growing a so-called "deep state."

In a mafia state, official *institutions of power voluntarily yield their power and authority to informal groups.* As a result, on the one hand, no one is responsible for anything, and, on the other hand, someone without official authority is responsible. Responsibility for decision making is diluted in the depths of the mafia state, supported by unseen mechanisms of "negotiators," corruption, and phone calls to the right people. The question of "who decides this?" and the search for that person becomes key. In order to solve a problem, you have to find the phone number of the right person who can hash out a solution. Mob rules and practices are tightly interwoven with the mafia state's structure and mechanisms.

When it's unclear who's responsible for what, an army of crooks and conmen surfaces who sell municipal and state positions, from a local police department position to positions of governor, member of parliament, or state minister. Often, the person thus appointed has to "earn" the position with kickbacks or services to whomever helped him attain the post.

5. Hallmarks of a mafia state: violence

In a mafia state, the ruling clan has at its disposal the entire gamut of official instruments of state violence and coercion. Violence, including murder, becomes the primary way of dealing with an opponent or an enemy.

The judicial system, law enforcement, penal systems, and also the armed forces and security and intelligence agencies, in fact, work for the interests of the ruling mafia group and are instruments in its hands.

In order to achieve specific goals, *the mafia state shares the right to commit violence with informal structures,* enabling it to break or circumvent the law if needed. Informal militarized structures are formed, which help solve tasks both domestically and abroad.

Origins of the Mafia State in Russia

Before looking at how the mafia state operates in Russia now, let's look at recent history, where we shall see the origins of such a form of governance.

Putin's three components

The word "*piterskie*" (guys from St. Petersburg) has long had a multi-layered meaning. It does not mean simply residents of the city on the Neva River or people from there; it also means members of powerful criminal gangs that gained influence first throughout St. Petersburg and the Leningrad Region, then far beyond.

St. Petersburg has been called the "crime capital of Russia" and described as "gangster St. Petersburg" (long before the eponymous TV series solidified this nickname). It is also no accident that the high-profile case involving the Russian mob abroad – the so-called "Spanish case"[9] – involved St. Petersburg organized crime. In the 1990s, the mob played a significant role in many Russian cities, but St. Petersburg is a city with a population in the millions, the second most populous city in the country, with huge industrial capacities, sea ports, and proximity to the state border. It is also Russia's cultural capital and main tourism attraction.

---

9 https://www.bbc.com/news/world-europe-45907655.

In the 1990s, St. Petersburg had not only the usual head of executive power, the governor, but also a "nighttime governor" – the Tambov-Malyshev mob boss Vladimir Kumarin (Barsukov), nicknamed "Kum."[10]

It was no accident that Russia's main gangsters and its most prominent citizens came together in one place. All of them essentially derived from "the same sandbox," with one or more tightly interwoven clans with a common origin. This is one of Putin's main secrets, and it answers, to a large degree, the question that has been asked many times: Who is Mr. Putin?

Putin, and Putinism in general, has a triple origin. When Putin first became president, he liked saying that

---

10 https://www.spb.kp.ru/daily/26956.4/4009099/ [in Russian].

11 Igor Sechin (b. September 1960), chief of Vladimir Putin's staff in the mayor's office of St. Petersburg and in the Russian Government. He was a deputy prime minister of the Russian Federation, the president's deputy chief of staff. Currently, chairman of the board of directors of the oil company Rosneft.

12 Dmitry Medvedev (b. September 1965), close ally of Putin, who filled in for Putin as Russian president from 2008-2012 and served as prime minister between 2012 and 2020. Once reputed to have favored some liberal reforms and a modernization program, he currently is a fervid supporter of the war against Ukraine and advocate of anti-Western positions.

he is Anatoly Sobchak's student and successor. The St. Petersburg mayor/governor Sobchak's former team (Sechin,[11] Medvedev,[12] Gryzlov,[13] Kozak,[14] Chubais,[15]

---

13 Boris Vyacheslavovich Gryzlov (b. December 1950), a Russian politician who was the leader of the ruling United Russia Party. Currently he is serving as the Russian ambassador to Belarus. He served as the chairman of the State Duma from 2003 to 2011 and as interior minister from 2001 to 2003.

14 Dmitry Nikolayevich Kozak (b. November 1958), Russian politician who has served as the deputy Kremlin chief of staff since 24 January 2020. He previously served as the deputy prime minister of Russia from 2008 to 2020. He is a close ally of Putin, having worked with him in the St. Petersburg municipal administration.

15 Anatoly Borisovich Chubais (b. 1955); a member of the Yeltsin administration in the 1990s, he was an important figure in the privatization of the Russian economy. From November 1994 until January 1996, Chubais held the position of deputy prime minister for economic and financial policy in the Russian government. From July 1996 until March 1997, Chubais was the chief of the Russian Presidential Administration and involved in various economic and business endeavors. He resigned from his official positions after the Russian full-scale invasion of Ukraine and left Russia in 2022.

Gref,[16] Kudrin,[17] Mironov[18]) did, in fact, end up holding the top posts in the country.

There is a second Putin component: key posts in state-owned enterprises and security and intelligence agencies are held by his friends and colleagues from the KGB/FSB: Patrushev, Poltavchenko, Bortnikov, Chemezov, Tokarev and Cherkesov (Cherkesov died in 2022).

There is a third component that Putin never talks about, the athletic component. These are the people who worked out with Putin in the 1970s. In the 1990s, these same people, together with Putin, jointly appropriated the riches of post-Soviet St. Petersburg, and in the early 2000s, Putin helped some of them become multi-millionaires and even billionaires.

---

16 Herman Gref (b. February 1964), Russian politician and businessman. He was the Minister of Economics and Trade of Russia from May 2000 to September 2007. Currently, he is the CEO and chairman of the executive board of Sberbank, the largest Russian bank.

17 Aleksei Kudrin, deputy mayor for financial matters in Sobchak's government, subsequently Russia's finance minister (2000-2011). Since December 9, 2022, Corporate Development Advisor at Yandex.

18 Sergei Mironov (b. February 1953), head of the Just Russia – For Truth faction in the Russian parliament, speaker of the upper chamber, the Federation Council, from 2001-2011. A strong proponent of the war in Ukraine.

The media has talked considerably about this hidden component of Putin's power, but, when discussing a mafia state's roots and methods, it makes sense to organize the information that came to light at various times.

The mafia path: from tsekhoviki (underground factory operators) to kingpin parliament deputies

First, let's sketch the overall background picture, the atmosphere in which the "guys from St. Petersburg" rose to the heights of money and power. The metamorphosis that Russia underwent in the 1990s, aside from *perestroika* and economic transformation, was strikingly described by Stanislav Govorukhin, who later became Putin's chief-of-staff, a prominent member of Parliament from the United Russia party, and a main figure in Putin's National Front. But that would be 20 years later. Back in the 1990s, the young, clear-headed artist pithily appraised events in a book he wrote after the 1993 coup. The book, entitled *The Great Criminal Revolution*, attracted a great deal of attention. Govorukhin was the first to say that, in post-*perestroika* Russia, the mafia won. But the mafia's victory didn't happen overnight – it had been brewing for decades. Starting in the 1970s, when young Putin was working out joint locking techniques on tatami mats, the first mafia layer emerged – the so-called "*tsekhoviki*," creators of the first fake factories that made money from the shortages of various goods and products. Even back then, *tsekhoviki* corrupted law enforcers and started engaging in racketeering. As pointed out in Alexandr Maksimov's [Russian-language] book published in the late 1990s, *Who is Who in Russian Crime*,[19] the first big racketeering ring formed in the 1970s, subsisting off of the first underground businessmen. This was the Mongol gang, where the later-infamous thief-in-law Yaponchik (the Japanese) (Ivankov) was a young "apprentice." The first big get-together of *tsekhoviki* from all over the USSR took place in 1979 in the resort town of Kislovodsk [North Caucasus]. At this conference, a directive was issued to set up a slush fund [Russ. *obshchak*],replenished with tithing from money extorted from underground businessmen. Not until 15 years later would this be called "racketeering."

Before Soviet people knew what a "thief-in-law"[20] was, a large-scale conference of thieves-in-law took place in Tbilisi [Georgia] in 1982, and the first underground armed groups were formed in Georgia and other Soviet republics of the Transcaucasus region.

Of course the security forces knew all about this. Deep inside the Soviet KGB, the first anti-organized crime

---

19 https://www.rulit.me/books/rossijskaya-prestupnost-kto-est-kto-read-71537-1.html [in Russian].

20 Thieves-in-law ("vory v zakone"): greatly respected high-ranking members of the underworld. This phenomenon formed in the USSR in the1930s, it's marked by a strict code of criminal traditions and is highly secretive.

program (still classified) was drafted. The *chekists*[21] got ever more intel about *criminal protection outfits*[22] *merging with Communist party leadership* [nomenclature]. For example, Georgia's Communist Party Central Committee future First Secretary Jumber Patiashvili gave away the bride at thief-in-law Kuchuuri's wedding. Operative sources said that Kuchuuri allegedly got so brazen as to order a hit on Gorbachev (the failed hitman Teimuraz Abaidze was arrested in May 1987).

By the late 1980s, the Soviet Union already was divided into clear turf zones controlled by thieves-in-law and their "authorized representatives" – the smotryashchie – "enforcers." Behind each thief was a multi-functional staff. In addition to "enforcers," there were "*polozhentzy*" (deputies), "brigadiers" (heads of gang "battalions"), "cashiers" (holders of the slush funds), and "fighters" (also called "infantrymen") – low-level thugs and racketeers).

Notably, all this existed long before the authorities allowed Russian citizens to engage in business. In the 1990s, *the mafia fused ever closer with the political elite.* Citizens learned about this mostly from crime reports.

---

21 Originally, "chekist" meant a staffer of the All-Russian Extraordinary Commission on Combating Counter-Revolution and Sabotage ("Vserossiskaya Chrezvychaynaya Komissiya po borbe s kontrevolutziyei I sabotazhem (VChK"), which existed 1917-1922). In a broader sense, this is a nickname for staffers of national security agencies that became CheKa successors.

22 Russian uses the word "*krysha*" or "roof" to signify criminal protection.

State Duma (parliament) members were getting killed one after the other. The mob managed to get the criminal businessman Andrey Dainisovich Aizderdzis elected to the State Duma, but when he refused to pay kickbacks, they killed him. The head of "Leninskaya OCG (organized crime group)" Frantz became assistant to a parliamentary deputy from the LDPR (Liberal Democratic Party of Russia) faction. The media often mentioned billionaire Parliament member Andrei Skoch in the same breath as the Solntsevo gang;[23] and in the mid-2010s, Skoch was also mentioned in connection with another scandal, the "Shakro case" scandal.

At the time, the LDPR became a party and a faction of gangsters. Within the faction, the St. Petersburg group was made up of mobsters headed by Mikhail Glushchenko, who admitted[24] ordering the hit on Galina Starovoitova on Kum's (Kumarin's) direct orders.

By 1999, Vladimir Zhirinovsky got so bold as to put mobsters on the top-10 of his election list. This included Krasnoyarsk mob boss Tolya Byk (the Bull) (Anatoly Bykov, who at one point controlled the Krasnoyarsk Aluminum Plant). The usually nonplussed Kremlin

---

23 Solntsevo—most notorious Russian crime syndicate, formed in Moscow in the late 1980s. After the fall of the Soviet Union, they reinforced their position by establishing contacts with politicians. By the late 1990s, they penetrated the banking business, which enabled them to launder their money. They have also operated in Europe and the U.S. and reportedly are still active in Russia

24 https://www.svoboda.org/a/29867519.html [in Russian].

leadership nevertheless decided this was too much, and the list was removed, although the candidates were allowed quickly to reapply, and the LDPR faction stayed in the Parliament.

GANGSTER SILOVIKI AND WEREWOLVES IN UNIFORM

Even back then, the mafia seeped into the FSB, despite the FSB's proclaiming itself as the main fighter of corruption and political crime. This was described in detail by State Duma deputy and *Novaya Gazeta* investigative journalist Yuri Shchekochikhin.[25] His 1996 article "The Cloak and Dagger Brotherhood" became a sensation, although these days such revelations would surprise no one.

Since then, the FSB's ties with crime groups keep resurfacing: one example is the Customs Office protection racket case, known as the "Three Whales" case. Recently, the FSB's ties with the mob came up in the case against Ivan Golunov, who had investigated the FSB's involvement with the cemetery mob.[26]

The mob took root in the Interior Ministry, too, with former and current police officers often committing crimes together with gangsters. In the late 1990s – early 2000s, we often heard the term "werewolves in uniform," although now it is no longer used.

---

25 Yuri Shchekochikhin was a State Duma deputy, journalist, author, screenwriter, *Novaya Gazeta* deputy chief editor; he died in 2003 of severe general intoxication. Some say he was poisoned with thallium, but according to other people, he died of alcohol intoxication.

26 https://navalny.com/p/6152/ [in Russian].

Putin and His Athletic Friends

Government officials and the crime world developed a relationship through athletic ties and sports foundations, as evidenced, for example, in the *Rossiya* TV March 19, 2013 broadcast of Arkady Mamontov's *Special Correspondent* primetime show. The topic of that episode was corruption in the housing sector, and it showed unique footage of the birthday celebration of St. Petersburg's "nighttime governor" Kum (Kumarin).[27] Mamontov later said that he got the flash drive with the video of the milestone celebration from All-Russian State Television and Radio Broadcasting Company general manager Oleg Dobrodeev's reception area. The recording was seized in 2007 during a search at Kumarin's St. Petersburg apartment on Tavricheskaya Street, and was kept in Investigative Committee head Alexandr Bastrykin's safe.

On the screen, we saw the birthday celebrant's honored guests: the head of Solntsevo mob Mikhas, former St. Petersburg deputy governor Yuri Antonov, who, after retiring, went to work at the St. Petersburg Fuel Company, which was controlled by the Tambov mob. Then there were close-ups of guests sitting at a separate table: Leonid Zelensky, Vladislav Kosenko, Konstantin Goloshchapov, and his wife. At the time of filming, Golosh-

---

27 (7) https://medium.com/@tzurrealism/massazhist-putina-6ae4bf6baf2f [in Russian].

chapov, known in the media as "Putin's masseur," was the business partner of Arkady Rotenberg. Together with Rotenberg, Goloshchapov co-founded SMP Bank and was planning to establish the "Russian Athos Society" jointly with presidential plenipotentiary envoy for the Central Federal District Georgy Poltavchenko and the very same Kum (Kumarin).

The St. Petersburg top mob boss's birthday celebration guests – Leonid Zelensky, Vladislav Kosenko, Konstantin Goloshchapov and Arkady Rotenberg – are Putin's old friends and sambo/judo sparring partners. They all trained in sambo in St. Petersburg in the 1970s. By the 1990s, these sambo clubs became security companies, protection outfits, intimidation gangs and debt collectors.

These people are further linked by their common trainers, whose influence is seen in, for example, the famous footage from 2013 of Putin arriving in St. Petersburg at the funeral of his first trainer Anatoly Rakhlin. After the ceremony, Putin unexpectedly broke away from his entourage and walked off alone in an unknown direction. This unexpected act showed how important the trainer had been in Vladimir Putin's coming of age.

Whereas Putin sometimes mentioned Rakhlin, he avoided mentioning his second trainer and instructor, Leonid Usvyatsov, for obvious reasons: Usvyatsov spent much of his life, about 20 years, behind bars. A father figure and unquestioned authority to young athletes, Usvyatsov introduced many of them to the Leningrad [(now St. Petersburg)] crime world and thieving practices.

Photographs from Usvyatsov's grave that surfaced in the media drew a great deal of attention. His tombstone bears an inscription that Usvyatsov himself devised. The epitaph is quite eloquent: "I am dead, but the mafia is immortal."[28]

---

28 https://tvrain.tv/teleshow/piterskie/ja_umer_no_bessmert-na_mafija-453004/ [in Russian; quotation from the second episode of the Russian documentary serial *Piterskie*].]

The Tambov mob comes to power

In the course of an investigation of the "Spanish case," an apartment was located on Kammenny Ostrov (Stony Island) in central St. Petersburg that belonged to the main person named in the case – Gennady Petrov. Most of Petrov's neighbors in the building were members of the famous *Ozero* (Lake) cooperative.[29] The high-rise was built by the Baltic Construction Company, which is tied to Gennady Petrov's son Anton Petrov (who was also declared an international fugitive). Petrov-Jr.'s business partner at Baltic Construction Company was Bank *Rossiya*, used by Putin's closest friends.

What links Putin's friends to the Tambov mob, and how did they come to be partners and neighbors? Former businessman Maksim Freidzon (who sued Gazprom and Lukoil for over $543 million) gave an interview to journalist Roman Bodanin for the third episode of the film "*Piterskie*" [Guys from St. Petersburg)].[30] In the interview, Freidzon related that, by 1996, the city's entire fuel and gas station sector was subordinate to the St. Petersburg mob bosses (in Russian: *avtoritety* or

---

29 https://tvrain.tv/teleshow/piterskie/piterskie_svoi-462188/ [in Russian; information from the third episode, "Wolves in Sheep's Clothing" of the Russian documentary serial *Piterskie*].

30 Loc. cit.

authorities), chiefly, the Tambov mob. The mob got this power with support from city hall, where deputy mayor Vladimir Putin oversaw liaisons with official and unofficial *siloviki*.

In the 1990s, both Petrov and his Baltic Bunkering Company business partner Ilya Traber (who is also considered Putin's old friend) joined the fuel and port business. Traber is nicknamed "the Antiquarian" for amassing his initial wealth by reselling luxury items.

In 1996, Putin, as Sobchak's second-in-command, leased Pulkovo airport's only fueling facility to a company called Sovex. In an interview to *Dozhd* (Rain) TV station,[31] Freidzon said that, in exchange for such a lucrative decision, Putin asked for 15% of Sovex, but they compromised at 4%. A year later, Sovex' annual profit was $600 million, and Freidzon says he was forced out.

Soon thereafter, essentially all St. Petersburg fuel facilities were controlled by the mob: Sovex fueled planes at Pulkovo airport, Traber's and Petrov's Baltic Bunkering Company bunkered ships in the port, while Traber-controlled Petersburg Fuel Company (PTK) supplied fuel to all public transport in town.[32]

When Putin's career took off, and he left St. Petersburg for Moscow, Alexander Dyukov was appointed to manage the terminal. Today, Diukov is head of Gazprom Neft, but back then he was an engineer at Sovex.

---

31 Loc. cit.

32 Loc. cit.

After Putin moved to Moscow, Aleksey Miller (who was under the mob boss Traber the Antiquarian at the time), was in charge of the port, Freidzon said.

Another partner of Traber's was Vladislav Reznik (Reznik and Traber founded "Russian Video"). Later, Reznik co-founded the United Russia Party, and was a longtime head of the State Duma Banking Committee. At one time, Reznik was considered a power broker among the ruling party.

Traber's influence was extensive. For example, sometime after 2010, while one of Putin's *dachas* (summer/vacation home) was under construction on a Vyborg region island, it was Traber's man, former Vyborg region head Georgy Poryadin, who drove Putin to the construction site.[33]

Mobsters from the 1990s did their best to conceal their shares in legitimate business using offshores and numerous shell companies. It was not until January 2022, in his first interview in 30 years to the Petersburg online news source *Fontanka*,[34] that Traber admitted creating the Petersburg Fuel Company, and he said that to this day he makes up to $1 billion per year. During the same interview, however, Traber noted that, per the recent ruling by one of the St. Petersburg courts, any charges against him alleging ties with crime groups are

---

33 https://www.yuga.ru/news/420197/ [in Russian]

34 https://www.fontanka.ru/2022/01/17/70371956/ [in Russian].

false. In the interview, "the Antiquarian" asserts that he set up the $1 billion business with honest work.

"Guys from St. Petersburg" and "the President's guys" are interconnected, and we see numerous confirmations of this. For example, the media reported that "Federation" Foundation head Vladimir Kiselev and his business partner, White Nights Festival[35] general manager Sergei Drapkin's ties with the underworld were exposed.[36] According to the media, Kiselev and Drapkin were once detained by St. Petersburg crime fighters on the charges that, in June 1992, while managing the White Nights Festival, they bought four million rubles worth of goods from the Tambov mob for the purpose of resale. Those goods had been obtained illegally. Naturally, the case was swept under the rug. In late 2010, the entire country learned that Kiselev and Putin were acquainted, when Kiselev's Federation Foundation put on a grandiose benefit concert in St. Petersburg. Not only did Putin attend the concert, but he also performed a classic American blues song while the public applauded. Putin had never before sung in public, let alone in English. Naturally, this performance attracted the attention of the Russian media, which was still partly independent at the time The media soon learned that Kiselev had links to the Tambov mob. This caused an uproar, and Putin never again publicly performed at Kiselev's events.

---

35 The St. Petersburg White Nights pop music festival was created in 1992 under Mayor Anatoly Sobchak's patronage.

36 https://novayagazeta.ru/articles/2012/02/24/48437-basmannyy-sud-vzyalsya-za-staroe [in Russian].

An unexpected prediction

In 1994, Yegor Gaidar, after leaving his post as First Deputy Prime Minister, was busy writing his book *Days of Defeat and Victory*.[37]

In it, he wanted to warn Russia about a possible future, although he had no intention of being a prophet. At the time, the 1993 Constitution had already been adopted, putting in place the prerequisites for an authoritarian regime; yet few imagined the direction in which Russia was actually heading. Gaidar's warning turned out to be the most accurate description of Russia's path: *The alliance of mafia and corruption in the early days of capitalism can produce an awful hybrid that Russian history has probably never known. This would truly be completely apocalyptic: an omnipotent mafia state, a real octopus. Let's keep in mind that a government official is always potentially more prone to crime than a businessman. A businessman can enrich himself honestly as long as no one stands in his way. A government official can get rich only dishonestly. The bureaucratic apparatus thus has many more mafia traits than do the business circles. And the framework of the bureaucratic system (including the penal system) can easily become the framework of a mafia system; it's all a matter of what goals it seeks to achieve. It's quite obvious what kind of a state can be built on statist principles (in reality, not*

---

37 Yegor Gaidar, *Days of Defeat and Victory* (Seattle, University of Washington Press, 1991); published in Russian in 1997.

in words) – a corrupt, criminal, semi-colonial state. Society becomes the state's colony, and, under such a regime, the menacing state itself becomes the colony of the mafia, both domestic and international mafia, which easily penetrates all of the apparatus' pores.[38]

Gaidar was one of the first to describe Russia as a "mafia state." The foundations of this system were being laid while Gaidar was still in office. His prediction was not heeded by the Russian democrats or by Boris Yeltsin's appointees, who carried out the first economic reforms in Russia in the early 1990s together with Yeltsin. At the time, considering that macroeconomics was more important, they focused on it, handing over political processes to *siloviki* and the bureaucratic apparatus, and giving free rein in the lowest economic processes to thugs, crime groups, and *siloviki*. This tangled web gave rise to the mafia state. As a result, liberals who had integrated into the system by the beginning of the 2000s helped sustain the mafia state economically. This did not, however, save either Russia or some of the liberals (such as Anatoly Chubais) from emigration and/or criminal prosecution. Liberals outside the system became enemies, while liberalism itself became demonized. To a great degree, this was a consequence of the erroneous policies of those very same liberals and democrats of the 1990s.

---

38 The citation is a translation of the Russian text.

The structure of the Russian mafia state

In the center of the mafia state structure is a group of the main beneficiaries of this form of governance. This group, the *mafia clan*, is the main internal level, the mafia state's core.

On the surface is the *pseudo-state*, which serves two functions: (1) *creating the appearance of a state* with instruments and institutions, and (2) *serving the clan's interests.*

Most Russian mafia clan members amassed their wealth during Vladimir Putin's rule because of their closeness to him, exploiting the state in their own interests. Their assets may be publicly visible or totally concealed. In any case, their personal income, even income reported publicly, is just part of the total capital the clan controls. The mafia's money flows through complicated layers of money laundering, and the total capital is hidden from the public's eye.

Some of the wealthiest individuals, whose wealth-building began in the 1990s, were able to develop a relationship with the mafia clan that allowed them to retain and increase their wealth – in exchange for loyalty and funding the mafia state's political projects.

Russia's mafia clan now controls practically all the key branches of the economy – primarily, the fuel and energy complex, the main source of income prior to the

February 2022 full-scale invasion of Ukraine. The mafia clan is a conglomeration of businessmen, security, intelligence, and law enforcement workers, and government officials who subordinate the entire state apparatus to their interests.

No matter how we classify these people, the insiders always remain the same. Let's identify several groups based on the type of their relationship with and closeness to the president.

Friends: (childhood friends, college friends, and *Ozero* (Lake)[39] cooperative members) – Arkady Rotenberg, Gennady Timchenko, Sergei Roldugin, Vladimir Yakunin, Yuri Kovalchuk, Nikolai Shamalov, Aleksandr Bastrykin, Konstantin Goloshchapov, Petr Kolbin, Viktor Khmarin.

Colleagues and work acquaintances: colleagues from the KGB or the FSB: Nikolai Tokarev, Sergei Chemezov, Sergei Ivanov, Nikolai Patrushev, Aleksandr Bortnikov, Sergei Naryshkin. Colleagues from St. Petersburg city hall or acquaintances made during that period: Dmitry Medvedev, Anatoly Chubais, Aleksey Miller, Aleksey Kudrin, Igor Sechin, Viktor Zubkov, Herman Gref, Dmitry Kozak, Vitaly Mutko, Sergei Mironov, Ilya Traber, Vladimir Litvinenko.

Acquaintances made in post-St. Petersburg days who became closest to the president through ties to his friends or gained his trust in another way. They are:

---

39 *Ozero* is a country home community founded by Vladimir Putin and his friends in 1996 in Leningrad Region.

Defense Minister Sergei Shoigu, who headed the Office of Emergency Management under Yeltsin and co-founded the United Russia party. Ramzan Kadyrov, who came to power in Chechnya after his father Akhmat Kadyrov's assassination in 2004. Then there are Gazprombank head Igor Akimov, VTB Bank head Andrey Kostin, and Russian Direct Investment Fund head Kirill Dmitriev. There is also a sub-group of trusted bodyguards who are "insiders" and, instead of guarding the president, carry out special tasks in various areas. They are: Aleksei Dyumin, Viktor Zolotov, Dmitry Mironov, Evgeny Zinichev (died in 2021), Sergei Morozov, and others.

Then there are *the president's relatives*. First, his daughters that he has yet to acknowledge officially – Katerina Tikhonova and Maria Faassen. The list apparently also includes: Alina Kabayeva[40]; Putin's first cousin once removed Mikhail Putin; Putin's former wife Lyudmila Putina (whose last name is now Ocheretnaya), Putin's purported girlfriend from his St. Petersburg days Svetlana Krivonogikh and her daughter; Putin's distant relative Anna Tsivileva and her husband, Kemerovo region Governor Sergei Tsivilev.

---

40 Alina Kabayeva is an Olympic champion in rhythmic gymnastics. The media have long hinted at her personal ties to Vladimir Putin and her being the mother of several of Putin's children, although none of this has been officially confirmed.

“Service staff”

One of the mafia state’s external levels is the “service staff,” the mafia state’s service mechanism. This stratum is extensive: it includes the entire bureaucratic machine adapted to serve the mafia group’s interests. Individuals who are part of this mechanism receive income thanks to the mafia state, but their role is one of service. They are paid for services rendered in tangible or non-tangible, official or unofficial form.

“Service staff” are part of the mafia group; they share its ideology and protect its interests, enabling the mafia to continue receiving income for as long and as safely as possible. In return, “service staff” receive direct remuneration as well as the ability to receive income through their own, often not quite legal, activity. This is why the *service staff is also interested in Russia’s remaining a mafia state as long as possible.*

The “service staff’s” main capital is proximity to the main *mafiosi* community. Their work is evaluated, and remuneration depends on their loyalty and the mafia group’s assessment of the results of their work. While mafia group members are essentially untouchable, “service staffers” are not immune to criminal prosecution because they are not full mafia “insiders.” Working as the mafia’s service staff isn’t about the salary – most important here are the informal incentives.

The “service staff” can be divided into several main groups:

The "state simulation" group

The mafia state needs constantly to substantiate its legitimacy and create the appearance of a healthy state system. 'Without such cover, a mafia group's activity would be very limited at the state level. Coordination occurs, first of all, at the presidential administration level, headed by head of the Administrative Directorate of the President[41] head Anton Vaino, and followed by Vaino's first deputies Sergei Kirienko and Aleksey Gromov, and State Duma speaker Vyacheslav Volodin. Also in this group are the government, the Central Bank, the Russian Central Electoral Commission, and opposition that's part of the system: the KPRF (Communist Party of the Russian Federation), the LDPR, the Just Russia Party, and the New People Party that joined the system later.

In this same group, we can include a pool of Putin's so-called technocrats: these are groups of federal and regional-level officials who made careers during Putin's rule; they have professional or managerial ambitions but no political ambitions. This is basically the entire government machine, which is subordinate to and exploited by the mafia community. Whereas mafia leadership remains largely unchanged, the technocrat group membership can be overhauled completely, but this will make no difference in the nature of this group or how it functions.

---

41 The Administrative Directorate of the President is a government entity that ensures the Russan President's operations and oversees the implementation of his decisions.

The "Protectors"

The regime protectors' objectives are: fighting dissen t, justifying the mafia's actions, ensuring long-term and safe income, and power preservation. All this maximally facilitates preserving the regime. [Below are several types of "protectors":]

The security, intelligence, and law enforcement bloc (*siloviki*)

The dominance of any authoritarian structure, whether a military *junta*, a communist party, or a mafia community, is impossible without a powerful repressive apparatus. *In a mafia state, the security, intelligence, and law enforcement agencies are no longer institutions ensuring the safety and security of the state and its citizens; they become similar to organized crime groups that, while competing with each other, serve the mafia.* In a mafia community, the security, intelligence, and law enforcement bloc has the distinguishing features of individual groups serving the mafia that replaced the state and instituted its own rules. There is a complicated relationship of cooperation and competition within the *siloviki* bloc.

Historically, the FSB has played a leading role in the Russian mafia state, first of all, as the successor to the KGB. Second, Putin and a significant number of mafia community members came from the organization. Third, the FSB is a security, intelligence, and law enforcement entity that often sees itself as being above the law if need be.

Falling within this category are all security, intelligence and law enforcement agencies (the *siloviki*) and their leadership: the Russian Foreign Intelligence Service (Russian acronym: SVR), the General Prosecutor's Office, the Investigative Committee, the Russian National Guard, the Interior Ministry, the Federal Penal Administration, and some Ministry of Defense subdivisions.

Policymaking

An important part of imparting legitimacy to the mafia community's actions is establishing a mafia legal system. *State laws are replaced by mafia laws,* and this becomes the norm.

This bloc performs the following tasks:

- *political* – persecuting and punishing ideological opponents and opposition members and putting in place guarantees for the mafia to stay in power as long as possible;
- *economic* – creating conditions for expropriating property in the group's interests; ensuring unhampered income with minimal expenditure, and legalizing the income. Here, the law becomes the main instrument.
- One of the bloc's groups – the legislative group – creates the necessary instruments, while another

group – the judicial group – applies and utilizes them. The first group's foundation is the United Russia Party faction in the State Duma, State Duma speaker Vyacheslav Volodin, and the Parliament's upper chamber – the Federation Council headed by speaker Valentina Matvienko. The second group includes Russia's entire court system. *The courts become part of the conveyor belt that arbitrarily handles the law in the mafia group's interests.*

"Special contractors"

These people are close to the clan and are used to carry out semi-legal or illegal tasks and unofficial missions when official government resources cannot be used. These people are not close enough to Putin to become "insiders" and clan members. Rather, they are effective "hirelings" who provide certain services in exchange for remuneration and special authority.

One such special contractor was Yevgeny Prigozhin, who was often called "Putin's chef." Knowing how to serve, listen, and be silent are the main skills Prigozhin was able to sell when first starting out as a "special contractor." Prigozhin's activities, however, were often mired in scandals, including the deaths of hired guns in Syria, the murder of Russian journalists in Africa, discovery of a troll factory, and Wagner Group staffer and former prisoner Nuzhin's murder with a sledgehammer.[42] Prigozhin's biography embodies the life of a person outside norms, rules, and laws. The Wagner Group that Prigozhin founded started playing a leading role during Russia's military action in Ukraine. By spring 2023, Prigozhin had managed to become one of the chief mouthpieces of not only the so-called "special military operation" but also of Russian policy as a whole. He was the only person still living in Russia who loudly and publicly criticized Defense Minister Sergei Shoigu, Russian army generals, and the course of the fighting. His rhetoric was directed against the "fat Russian elite" and "national traitors." Essentially, he represented the "angry patriots" – a group of right-wing conservatives espousing nationalistic, patriotic views (i.e., anti-Western) and demanding greater militarization, more decisive action on the frontlines, and placing the country on a war footing. All that ended when Prigozhin and other Wagner Group leaders were killed in a plane crash on August 23, 2023, just two months after Prigozhin's "march for justice" toward Moscow, during which he demanded the removal of Shoigu and Chief-of-Staff Gerasimov.

Another noteworthy "service staffer" of the ruling regime is Vladislav Surkov, whose services to the mafia clan were primarily in the area of ideology. He ham-

---

42 On July 30, 2018, three Russian journalists (Orhan Jemal, Aleksandr Rastorguyev and Kirill Radchenko) were murdered in the Central African Republic where they came to investigate the Wagner group's activities.

mered out the ideological base of Putinism, cleaned up the Russian political sphere, and put in place an internal system of censorship and propaganda.

Surkov authored numerous concepts that camouflaged the political regime, starting from the idea of "sovereign democracy" through the "isolation of a half-breed nation" to Putinism's universal greatness.

Surkov developed the ideology for Vladimir Putin's first terms in office: "stabilizing the political system" during the first term, and "fighting the oligarchs" during the second term. He also called the power construct during Dmitry Medvedev's presidency a "tandem."[43]

In September 2013, Surkov became the Russian president's assistant on the development of Abkhazia and South Ossetia. However, Surkov's primary task was carrying out missions, including covert missions in Ukraine. Putin authorized Surkov to interact with representatives of the Ukrainian leadership and local Ukrainian elite on a wide range of issues. In early 2014, during Euromaidan, Surkov engaged in "secret" diplomacy as the Russian president's representative in Ukraine. During that time, Surkov made several visits to Viktor Yanukovich in Kyiv. According to the Ukrainian General Prosecutor's Office, the purpose of Surkov's trips was to gather information about the nature of the protest movements, their organization and their financing.

---

43 https://www.znak.com/2018-05-15/zloy_geniy_rossiyskoy_politiki_vladislav_surkov_pokidaet_kreml_ili_ne_sovsem [in Russian].

Surkov coordinated not only the ideological part of the operation but also the money flows through Donbas. This is indirectly confirmed in an interview with former FSB worker and political figure Igor Strelkov[44]: "Unfortunately, those involved with Novorossiya[45] issues inside Russia, who are authorized to do so – in particular, the infamous Vladislav Yurievich Surkov – are people whose only intent is to destroy; they provide no real, actual help. Specifically, V. Yu. Surkov brilliantly demonstrated this in South Ossetia and other regions. Wherever he went, property was carved up and looted instead of any real help being provided."[46]

---

44 Strelkov, pseudonym for Igor Girkin, is a hardline nationalist who led the Russian-backed separatists in Ukraine in 2014. He has accused Putin of weakness in the present war and is presently in custody in Moscow, awaiting trial on charges of extremism.

45 Novorossiya was the historical term used in the period of the Russian Empire to describe the area that later became the southern area of Ukraine. The term was dropped in the Soviet era. In order to emphasize the area's historic connection to Russia, Putin reintroduced the term in 2014. The attempt, in May 2014, to establish a modern confederation of Novorossiya consisting of the self-proclaimed Donetsk People's Republic and the Luhansk People's Republic ultimately failed.

46 http://novorossiia.ru/main/13879-g-n.html [in Russian].

"The Preachers"

This group's objective is to influence public opinion in order to secure loyalty to the regime – meaning a positive view of the very nature of the state and the specific individuals in power. After the full-scale invasion of Ukraine on February 24, 2022, this group's main task is ideological support for the so-called "special operation."

In a post-communist mafia state such as Russia, a *synthesis is attained out of the USSR's totalitarian propaganda experience, criminal culture, conspiracy theories, and the population's high degree of religiosity*. This bloc therefore consists of media managers, state propagandists, and leaders of Russia's main religious denominations. Here, we can identify five main groups:

- staff propagandists;
- officials, owners, and staff of pro-Kremlin media;
- political and PR consultants working for the Kremlin;
- religious figures;
- cultural figures.

The list of official media bigwigs numbers dozens. The most prominent among them are heads of TV stations and TV companies, such as Channel One general manager Konstantin Ernst, All-Russian State Television and Radio Broadcasting Company general manager Oleg Dobrodeev, NTV general manager Aleksey Zemsky, former NTV general manager and All-Russian State Television and Radio Broadcasting Company general manager's advisor Vladimir Kulistikov, RT editor-in-chief Margarita Simonyan, RT general manager Aleksei [elsewhere "Aleksey"; choose one for consistency] Nikolov, and *Rossiya Segodnya* (Russia Today) news agency general manager Dmitry Kiselev. Some of them are propagandists as well.

The official propagandists: Vladimir Solovyev, Mikhail Leontyev, Katerina Andreeva (who hosts Channel One news), hosts of 60 Minutes on Rossiya-1 TV channel Yevgeny Popov and Olga Skabeeva, Channel One anchors Kirill Kleimenov, Petr Tolstoy, Valery Fadeev, Evgeny Satanovsky, Aleksei Pushkov, Anton Krasovsky, Yakov Kedmi, and others.

Another group within this bloc that serves Putin's regime are political consultants, political scientists, and PR consultants. In particular: Civil Society Development Foundation director Konstantin Kostin and his wife Olga; Surkov's longtime colleague and political consultant Aleksey Chesnakov, *Mikhailov and Partners* PR agency founder Sergei Mikhailov (who later became general manager of ITAR-TASS state information agency), *Apostol* (Apostle) media agency founder Tina Kandelaki, IMA Group head Andrei Gnatiuk, Russian Public Opinion Research Center general manager Valery Fedorov, and others.

The third group are religious figures, primarily Russian Orthodox Church members headed by Patriarch Kirill. Patriarch Kirill speaks out directly in support of Putin and calls on his congregation to avoid taking part in opposition campaigns.[47] Patriarch Kirill displayed special "political instructor" qualities during combat in Ukraine. In his sermons, instead of calling for peace, he called on his flock to consolidate and enlist.

The fourth group are the numerous individuals from Russian cultural circles who are very involved in the government's political projects. They are the emotionally charged intermediaries between those in power and the masses. They were all drafted into action during the "special operations" period. Standing out among them is the singer Shaman beloved by the powers; "old guard" Oleg Gazmanov and Nikolai Rastorguev, Grigori Leps, Evgeny Petrosyan, Denis Maidanov, Vika Tsyganova, Yuliya Chicherina, and Vladimir Mashkov.

---

47 https://www.kommersant.ru/doc/1868593 [in Russian].

How the mafia state operates in Russia

By the time Vladimir Putin came to power, conditions in Russia were ripe for the speedy and easy building of the mafia state. The groundwork had already been laid during Boris Yeltsin's presidency. By then, the Soviet political and economic system had been dismantled, and the new was in the formative stage. Thus, there were no organizational, social, or political obstacles to the formation of a new state mechanism. In essence, the *Soviet totalitarian regime was transformed into a mafia state.*

After the collapse of the USSR, under Mikhail Gorbachev and Boris Yeltsin, the regime was devolving into the abuse of power, but it was not yet a true mafia state. Under Vladimir Putin, the system was fine tuned to its logical conclusion.

The mafia state's court system

In a mafia state, the judicial system serves the mafia clan's interests at both the federal and regional level, and judges are often directly involved in implementing the objectives of criminal, security/law enforcement, and bureaucratic groups, sometimes all merging into one whole.

Russian judges are well aware that they are part of the system – a system that utilizes the law more than it serves it.

Former judge of the infamous Basmanny Court Yelena Yarlykova describes this quite accurately: "You realize what the rules are almost from day one working at the court. On cases of any significance, you consult with the court chairperson, who consults with the Moscow City Court chairperson. And if you express your point of view, you are told: 'Think about yourself, your family, your child.' And there isn't much choice: you either do what you're told, or the next day you no longer work at the court, and you're lucky if you're allowed to resign."[48]

Judge Yarlykova convicted Yukos Affair defendants Vladimir Pereverzin and Vladimir Malakhovsky and sentenced them to 11 and 12 years in prison, respectively. She also ruled to arrest Vasily Aleksanyan.

The Yukos Affair was a patent manifestation of the essence of the mafia judicial system and its objectives. The judicial sys-

48 https://newtimes.ru/articles/detail/28961 [in Russian].

tem comprehensively serves the mafia group's political and economic interests. Igor Sechin, who at the time was deputy head of the presidential administration, is widely credited with initiating and organizing the Yukos Affair.[49] Sechin later became head of Rosneft, which obtained all of Yukos' main assets. Vladimir Putin's ideological opponent, [Yukos head] Mikhail Khodorkovsky received two criminal convictions and spent a total of 10 years in prison. The various courts and judges worked in coordination: some extended [pretrial] custody and convicted Khodorkovsky and his Yukos colleagues in criminal matters; others (arbitration courts) ruled in favor of the tax inspectorate that assessed Yukos with billions of rubles in tax debts.

Yukos is not the only example of criminal and arbitration courts working in tandem. One high-profile case (which did not end in a prison term) involved another asset that Rosneft wanted: Bashneft. In 2009, the *Sistema* [System] Joint-Stock Financial Corporation bought Bashneft. Five years later, *Sistema* founder and main shareholder Vladimir Yevtushenkov was summoned to the Investigative Committee for questioning as investigators wanted to know about this deal. A few months after the interrogation, Basmanny Court placed Yevtushenkov under house arrest on [criminal] charges of laundering property, that is, law enforcement agencies alleged that former owner Ural Rakhimov criminally obtained Bashneft from the Bashkir government.[50] At the same time, the Moscow Arbitration Court ruled that

---

49 https://www.kommersant.ru/doc/1006174 [in Russian].

50 https://tass.ru/proisshestviya/1465638?ysclid=lks2r0n-4kf112529756 [in Russian].

Sistema Joint-Stock Financial Corporation must return Bashneft to the state. After Bashneft was returned to the state, Yevtushenkov was released from house arrest. That's how criminal and commercial court proceedings are synchronized. A short while later, Bashneft became part of Rosneft as a result of "privatization."

People who become judges in Russia usually either come from law enforcement agencies or have spent years working for the courts, e.g., as judge's clerks, for low pay in the hopes of becoming a judge. As court staffers, they learn the rules, practices and inner workings of relationships in the system that they must heed if they want to become judges.

On paper, the [Russian] law on the status of judges and the Constitutional law on the Russian Federation judicial system state that the judicial branch is separate and acts independently from the legislative and executive branches.[51] However, federal judges in both general-jurisdiction and arbitration courts are appointed by the president on the recommendation of the Supreme Court chairperson. Constitutional Court judges are appointed by the Federation Council on the president's recommendation. Thus, the executive branch can directly influence the judicial branch through judicial appointments.

An indirect lever of pressure is the judges' remuneration. The difference between lower-court and higher-court judges' salaries is enormous. Former RF Consti-

---

51 http://letters.kremlin.ru/info-service/acts/19 [in Russian].

tutional Court judge Tamara Morshchakova explained this in an interview: “The low-level judge understands that, in order to advance, to achieve some kind of social upward mobility, he has to leave the bottom ranks and aim for the higher court.”[52]

In the court system, the judge is greatly dependent on the court’s internal hierarchy, the court leadership. Although the court system itself is not part of other hierarchies, court leadership does depend on those other hierarchies.

In this regard, the practice of “curatorship” is noteworthy. Judges have additional supervisors – the curators. For justices of the peace, it is the district judge; every district court is supervised by the regional court, and regional courts are supervised by the Supreme Court. These court overseers are not defined in the law, but their activity is described in internal rules. The curators have unofficial influence over court decisions. When a verdict or other judicial decision is appealed, the appeal most often lands on the desk of that particular judge’s “supervisor.”

In Russia, *siloviki* have a special relationship with the courts. The FSB’s “Department M” centrally oversees the judges,[53] actively influences judicial appointments, conducts wiretapping, and attends some court sessions

---

52 http://antipytki.ru/2016/11/24/sude-prihoditsya-vybirat-zashhishhat-pravo-ili-svoyu-kareru/ [in Russian].

53 https://www.proekt.media/research/nezavisimost-sudey/ [in Russian].

to see how trials are conducted. The FSB and other security and intelligence agencies, however are not the only ones controlling the courts. Others have "pocket" judges, too, for example, the Interior Ministry, the Investigative Committee and separate groupings within departments.[54] In 2010, sources told *The New Times* magazine that "judges are split into two groups: the first group is controlled by the FSB's "Department M" or Prosecutor's Office Investigative Committee investigators, and the Interior Ministry Investigative Committee investigators. The second group constitutes judges who, in obviously political cases, follow the lead of Moscow City Court chairperson Olga Yegorova, who, due to her status, does not depend on rank-and-file *chekists.*"[55] It's not just a matter of control – it is also a matter of connections, and the courts' serving the interests of other government system members.

In summer 2020, Moscow City Court chairperson Olga Yegorova resigned. She was probably the most controversial figure in Russian "justice." Her family could be deemed a model mafia state family: her husband was an FSB Lt. Gen. (he died in 2012), while her daughter reportedly worked for Rosneft. Yegorova headed the Moscow City Court for 20 years, starting in 2000. She was appointed to that post by Vladimir Putin's decree. This appointment may have been linked to Yegorova's ruling on the appeal of Tverskoy Intermu-

---

54 https://www.proekt.media/research/nezavisimost-sudey/ [in Russian].

55 https://newtimes.ru/articles/detail/21606[in Russian].

nicipal Court's decision finding unlawful the initiation of a criminal case against Vladimir Gusinsky. If Moscow City Court were to affirm the Tverskoy Court's decision, the General Prosecutor's Office would have had to recall Gusinsky's international arrest warrant and withdraw his extradition request. Under Yegorova's chairmanship, however, Moscow City Court overturned Tverskoy Intermunicipal Court's decision.[56] After that, Moscow City Court rulings were issued in line with the Kremlin's interests. As Moscow City Court chairperson, Olga Yegorova was able to influence heads of district courts. Sometimes this was done so blatantly that it caused a public uproar – for example, when, according to several sources and the court staff's public statements, Khamovnichesky Court judge Viktor Danilkin constantly reported to the Moscow City Court during Mikhail Khodorkovsky and Platon Lebedev's trial and received instructions from the Moscow City Court.[57] Yegorova is on the expanded Global Magnitsky Sanctions list; she refused the request of the mother of Sergei Magnitsky, jailed Hermitage Capital tax advisor, to let her son receive an independent medical expert evaluation, and she affirmed the Tverskoy Court's decision to keep Magnitsky in custody. Earlier, Magnitsky had said that Russian government officials and *siloviki* had devised a scheme for large-scale embezzlement of state funds through illegal tax refunds. In response, the gov-

---

56 https://www.kommersant.ru/doc/134443[in Russian].

57 https://www.bbc.com/russian/russia/2011/04/110415_yukos_trial_another_antidanilkin [in Russian].

ernment charged Magnitsky with abetting tax evasion, arrested him in 2008, and following serious health problems, he died in jail.[58]

The researcher Andrew Foxhall notes: "In a State where corruption lies at the very epicentre of power, all our assumptions about the operation of the rule of law are inverted. It is those running honest business ventures that are prosecuted. It is those who refuse to collaborate with corruption that find their businesses confiscated by court order. It is those who oppose the kleptocratic hegemony of the tiny group that maintains a stranglehold on power in Moscow that find themselves branded criminals, or become the losing party in major commercial litigation. It is those who speak out publicly against the regime that are targeted for assassination at home or abroad. Lawlessness has become the norm in Putin's Russia."[59]

Federal-level courts are dependent because judges are appointed by presidential decree. Regional-level courts are also dependent because judges are firmly integrated into the local elite's life. Finally, courts are simply prone to corruption.

A classic example of an independent and honest judge being expelled from the court system is the case

---

58 Magnitsky's death in prison in 2009 aroused an international outcry. In 2012, the U.S. passed the Magnitsky Act, which imposed sanctions on those reputedly involved in Magnitsky's death.

59 https://henryjacksonsociety.org/wp-content/uploads/2020/01/HJS-Russian-Influence-Report-web.pdf.

of Sergei Pashin who, along with some other judges, became a judge during the political thaw period of the early 1990s. For six years, Pashin was a member of the Presidential Council on Human Rights. According to *Russkiy Reporter* (Russian Reporter), Pashin was "one of those who introduced the jury system into Russia, and thanks to whom there is no death penalty."

Pashin, a law school graduate, first helped set up the court system in the new Russia, then worked in that system himself. In 1992, he became head of the Presidential State Legal Administration's judicial reform department (yes, there was such a department), and drafted the first laws regarding the courts. In 1995-1996, he helped pass those laws as deputy head of the State Duma Legal Department.

Pashin then spent five years at Moscow City Court, one of Russia's main bodies of the judicial system. From 1996 to 2001, he was a Moscow City Court judge under Olga Yegorova's predecessor and senior colleague Zoya Korneva (whom journalists called an "especially poisonous snake"). Korneva and her deputy Yegorova (who became head of Moscow City Court in 2000) eventually got rid of Pashin when his verdicts fell increasingly out of line with Yeltsin's later policies and Putin's early policies. Pashin was well-known for explaining his rulings in great detail (in contrast to his colleagues' superficial casuistry) as well as for his special rulings regarding officials.

At the time, the judicial branch was not yet fully controlled by the executive branch, and the Supreme Court reinstated Pashin. The Supreme Qualification Collegium of Judges also ruled in his favor. Nevertheless, in

2001, Pashin resigned and started teaching criminal law at Moscow universities. He always denied that he left because of a conflict with Olga Yegorova.

Another judge expelled from the Moscow City Court, Olga Kudeshkina, did talk about conflicts with chairperson Yegorova and Yegorova's vengefulness. Kudeshkina was trying the famous "Three Whales" case involving Customs Office smuggling and bribe-taking under the FSB's protection. Kudeshkina was about to convict Interior Ministry Investigative Committee investigator Pavel Zaitsev, who uncovered wrongdoings by *siloviki* but was charged with abuse of power. Kudeshkina's boss Yegorova did not like the direction in which the trial was heading. Kudeshkina said that Yegorova summoned her to her office several times, insisting Kudeshkina report to Yegorova on the court sessions. In the end, the case was reassigned to another judge, who convicted Zaitsev and imposed a two-year suspended sentence. In 2004, Kudeshkina, who exposed Yegorova, was stripped of her judge's status.

By that time, the judicial branch had been essentially fully "purged." Only the Constitutional Court still had a few dissenters, but their role was limited to special opinions. During the constitutional reform of 2020, those last dissenters were removed, and it became illegal to publish dissenting opinions.

Security and intelligence agencies in the service of the mafia state

It is the morning of August 20, 2020. An airplane flying from Tomsk to Moscow makes an emergency landing in Siberia's Omsk airport because a passenger suddenly fell ill. That passenger was opposition politician Aleksey Navalny. A while later, Navalny would be flown to Berlin, and several countries' laboratories would later determine that he had been poisoned with a chemical weapon of the *Novichok* [nerve agent] series. Later, an independent multinational journalists' investigation would find that the poisoning had been organized and perpetrated by current agents of the Russian FSB.[60]

This was not the first time a Russian opposition member had been poisoned. In 2015, Vladimir Kara-Murza, head of the Boris Nemtsov Foundation for Freedom, landed in the hospital for the same reason,[61] as did in 2018 Pussy Riot member Petr Verzilov.[62] In Aleksey Navalny's case, it was proven that the FSB was behind the crime.[63]

---

60 https://theins.ru/politika/237705 [in Russian].

61 https://www.currenttime.tv/a/27493037.html [in Russian].

62 https://www.bbc.com/russian/news-45559464 [in Russian].

63 https://navalny.com/p/6446/ [in Russian].

Let's revisit the events that preceded Vladimir Putin's election to Russia's top post – namely, the apartment building explosions in 1999.

In September 1999, a series of terrorist acts occurred in Moscow and in the cities of Buinaksk and Volgodonsk. At the same time, a strange discovery in the town of Ryazan drew the public's attention: a vigilant resident found bags of explosives and an unknown substance resembling hexogen in a residential building's basement. The Interior Ministry announced that a terrorist act had been averted. A day later, the FSB said that anti-terrorism exercises were being held in Ryazan. In early 2002, the book *Blowing up Russia* was published, co-authored by former FSB officer Aleksandr Litvinenko and historian Yuri Felshtinsky, Ph.D. The authors closely examine the theory that the FSB may have been behind what happened in Ryazan and possibly behind the building explosions in other cities.

Vladimir Putin gained popularity during the military campaign in Chechnya. At the time, he was prime minister (since August 1999). This support enabled him to win the presidential election in May 2000.

State Duma member and journalist Yuri Shchekochikhin also investigated who was behind the apartment building explosions. In 2002-2003, he was on the *Public Commission for Investigating the Circumstances of Building Explosions in Moscow and Volgodonsk and Exercises in Ryazan in September 1999.* Shchekochikhin died July 3, 2003 in Moscow as a result of an unknown rapidly progressing illness. The official cause of death was "acute general intoxication." In November 2006, *Blowing up Russia* co-author Alexandr Litvinenko died after being poisoned with a rare, hard-to-detect radioactive substance called Polonium-210.

Less than 6 months after Navalny's poisoning, most of the primary medics who treated him at the Omsk hospital where he was brought from the plane, left the hospital. Chief physician Aleksandr Murakhovsky (who made official statements to the media about Navalny's condition, asserting there was no evidence of poisoning) was appointed head of the Omsk Region health department.[64] His deputy Anatoly Kalinichenko resigned and went to work at a private clinic. Another deputy chief physician responsible for resuscitating and treating Navalny, Sergei Maksimishin, died in early February 2021, with heart attack as the official cause of death.

In January 2021, Navalny flew from Berlin back to Moscow, where he was arrested immediately after the plane landed and a series of criminal cases were opened. He was sentenced to nine years in a strict regime camp on the charge of large scale embezzlement. Then in August 2023, Navalny was sentenced to 19 years in a special regime forced labor camp on a charge of extremism. The prison conditions were close to torturous – Navalny was repeatedly sent to a punishment cell (in essence, a prison inside a prison) on the most varied trumped-up pretexts. In December 2023, he was secretly transferred to a prison in the settlement Kharp in Russia's far north,

---

64 Murakhovsky was removed from this position in fall 2023.

where severe weather conditions prevail. On 16 February 2024, it was announced that Aleksey Navalny died in the labor camp "of natural causes."

Evidently, under Vladimir Putin, Russia's *siloviki* stop at nothing. Security and intelligence agencies of the Russian mafia state continue the traditions and specific experience of the OGPU (Joint State Political Directorate)[65], the NKVD (People's Commissariat for Internal Affairs)[66], and the KGB. Soviet security and intelligence agencies traditionally sought to eliminate ideological leaders. Concurrently with the Great Terror [of the 1930s] in the Soviet Union, Soviet security and intelligence agencies carried out political assassinations abroad in order to eliminate "enemies of the people." In one such special operation in 1930, general Alexandr Kutepov, who was an active member of the White [anti-Bolshevik] Movement and chairman of the Russian All-Military Union, was kidnapped in Paris. The circumstances of his death are still unknown. In 1937, another White Movement general Evgeny-Ludwig Miller was kidnapped in Paris, brought to Moscow, and shot to death in 1939 in the NKVD's jail. A defector, former resident spy Grigory Arutyunov, was killed in Europe in 1937. After defecting, Arutyunov published an exposé, a book titled: *OGPU: Russia's Secret Terror* [under the

---

65 OGPU (JSPD) – Joint State Political Directorate, a special Soviet national security agency that existed 1923-1934.

66 NKVD – the USSR People's Commissariat for Internal Affairs.

pseudonym Agabekov]. Following the book's publication, hundreds of Soviet agents were arrested in Iran and other Middle Eastern countries, and the USSR's relations with Shah of Iran Reza Pahlavi sharply deteriorated. In August 1940, Lev Trotsky, one of the main political opponents during Stalin's rise to one-man power, was killed abroad [in Mexico]. These are just a few examples of the numerous murders carried out by Soviet security and intelligence agencies.

Mafiosi-style lawmaking

In a mafia state, the legislative branch does not operate in order to enact lawful, normative rules that apply to everyone and are monitored. Instead, the legislative branch becomes an *instrument of arbitrary lawmaking in the mafia group's interests.* As it controls all the highest state positions, the mafia group can amend the law to suit itself.

In Russia, the State Duma approves, initiates, and passes laws with a speed more reminiscent of a robotized conveyor belt than a state entity. This is why the legislative branch in Russia has been dubbed "the mad printer."

Over Putin's 20 years in power, legislation was rewritten, and the Constitution was amended despite promises not to do so. For example, in 2008, laws were amended extending the presidential term, and it was done at lightning speed: on November 11, 2008, then-president Dmitry Medvedev introduced a bill in the State Duma to amend the RF Constitution, increasing the presidential term from four to six years and extending the State Duma's authority from four years to five. By late November, the State Duma managed to adopt the bill in three readings, and by December 31, the law was published and took effect.

Conformity, which had become the norm back in the Soviet days and joint responsibility originating from mafia law made legislative miracles possible. In 2020, the State Duma approved Constitutional amendments on Vladimir Putin's initiative. Among them was an amendment that enables Vladimir Putin to run for president two more times. A year later, in early April 2021, Putin signed a new law modifying the law on elections and referendums to line up with the Constitutional amendments.

At the same time, the law governing elections was "cleaned up" once again. Earlier, in 2003, the law "On Elections for the RF President" was adopted, which created disparity in the ability to run for office between candidates nominated by political parties and electoral blocs, on the one hand, and self-nominees on the other hand. Candidates nominated by political parties can run without collecting any electoral signatures at all, whereas self-nominees now need at least 500 electoral signatures (up from 100), and two million voter signatures (up from one million). Election legislation then became even more restrictive. On July 12, 2006, voting "against all" was eliminated in all elections, as were the corresponding conditions for voiding an election. Moreover, the candidate nominating procedure was redefined: parties were now barred from nominating candidates from other parties, including those on candidates' lists.

Control over elections

In a mafia state, *elections serve to legitimize those in power. The mafia group views elections as confirming the mafia's right to power.* For this reason, the mafia state preserves the institution of elections despite its seeming senselessness. Elections become a "show of strength" of sorts and a way of checking the loyalty of the apparatus and of seeing how well the mafia's resources are mobilized in order to ensure victory.

A well-known political scientist Grigory Golosov explained precisely the nature of Russian elections in an interview: "From an instrumental point of view, elections [in general] are needed in order to punish or reward the current regime. Let's say you want to punish it, then you vote against it, realistically hoping for changes and for the current regime to end. In Russia, this is impossible. Regardless of what voters do, the very structure of the elections makes such an outcome impossible. For that reason, Russian elections do not fulfill the primary instrumental objective, and from that point of view they are a sham. At the same time, elections do serve other purposes, such as political mobilization, a demonstration of loyalty, power legitimization, and even citizens' emotional expression of willingness, because, for many, voting is a purely emotional act."

Electoral law and election process expert Andrei Buzin, who was a member of the Moscow Municipal Electoral Commission in a consultative capacity from 2001 to 2009, noted the following regarding the 2019 State Duma elections: "The Moscow elections clearly show that, during elections, our parties are just legal decorations, while the main election participant is the informal party of government officials. What's worse, this party isn't just a participant – it's also the organizer of the elections, with all the resulting consequences."[67] This is typical of Russian elections overall.

Essentially, elections are what Grigory Golosov called "*electoral measures*."[68] During preparatory stages, we see two complementary processes: blocking opposition candidates from running for office, and ensuring that target numbers are reached. Later, a third type of measures was added (after demonstrations calling for fair elections on Bolotnaya Square and Sakharov Avenue in Moscow after State Duma elections in December 2011): preventing post-election protests.

During Putin's 20 years in power in Russia, mechanisms were honed that bar non-system opposition members from running against regime candidates. Only official opposition that's part of the political system may take part in elections. The Central Electoral Commission blocks "wrong" candidates on various pretexts, such as: "insufficient electoral group;" "has lived in Russia less than 10 years;" "did not present min-

---

67 https://www.vedomosti.ru/opinion/articles/2019/07/24/807251-byurokratiya-manipuliruet [in Russian].

68 https://republic.ru/posts/1/785775 [in Russian].

utes of electoral meeting;" "presented too few signatures," or "failed to meet the signature filing deadline." And the most tried-and-true trick of professional politicians: rejecting signatures. But some tricks truly make the mind reel. For example, during the "tandem" special operation of 2008, a *Drugaya Rossiya* (Other Russia) coalition leader Garry Kasparov was blocked from running because the group that nominated him could not hold a conference. The reason the conference could not be held is that all conference venues refused to rent their spaces to the group.

Presidential elections of 2018 hold the record for the number of candidates barred from running: 29 candidates were either blocked or withdrew from the race for "failing to meet signature filing deadlines" or "violating how the nominating electoral group conference is held." Opposition member Aleskei Navalny was barred from running due to his "criminal" history.

State Duma elections are virtually identical to presidential elections. Parties that are already registered can still be barred from elections under various pretexts, while non-system opposition runs into roadblocks when even first attempting to register its party.

The groundwork for this was laid in 2001, with adoption of the law on political parties. That law specified the criteria for registering a political group as a party: the group must have regional divisions in at least half of the RF subjects, must have at least 10,000 members, and its headquarters, divisions and departments must be located in Russia.

All political actors in Russia were now forced to heed the new rules and try to somehow adapt to the system. Another barrier was put in place in order to bar new political players from running.

For example, starting in 2012, Aleksei Navalny and his allies made numerous attempts to register their party under various names: (*Narodny Alyans* (People's Alliance), *Partiya Progressa* (Party of Progress), and "*Rossiya Budushchego*" (Russia of the Future), but the Ministry of Justice rejected each attempt. The system also can de-register a party at any moment. For example, the Russian Supreme Court suspended the activities of the *Grazhdanskaya Initsiativa* (Civil Initiative) party, whose candidate Kseniya Sobchak ran for president. After it was announced that *Grazhdanskaya Initsiativa* was being renamed to *Partiya Peremen* (Party of Changes) led by Gudkov and Sobchak, however, the Ministry of Justice refused to register the changes.

Additional filters were put in place, starting with Duma elections of 2007. Furthermore, the majority system was abolished along with voting in single-member constituencies; parties were forbidden from forming electoral blocs; independent Russian monitors were forbidden (and only monitors from the parties were left in place). In 2007, 11 parties were able to take part in elections. The United Russia Party, whose federal list was headed by Putin, received 64.3% of votes and won 315 Duma seats. The RF Communist Party, LDPR and *Spravedlivaya Rossiya* (Just Russia) also joined the Duma, forming the Duma composition for years to come, with insignificant variation in the proportion of seats held.

A curious thing happened in the course of those elections: the United Russia Party did not participate in televised debates, and the time allotted to United Russia debates on TV was instead used to run free promos. United Russia had so much airtime that when the All-Russian Public Opinion Research Center conducted polls, 8% of Russians surveyed insisted that they saw United Russia members debating on TV with candidates from other parties. What's more, 69% of those who "saw" these debates found United Party candidates' arguments convincing.

Over the years, the mechanism of conducting sterile elections was honed and perfected. However, organizers of electoral campaigns were also tasked with ensuring voter turnout in order to make elections look legitimate. Here, the regime's main resource is mobilizing government workers and employees of state-owned enterprises. Here's how it's done: at the highest municipal level, city hall oversees elections.[69] City Hall decides which officials are responsible for voter turnout and election results in a specific state-funded area – say, in education. In turn, those individuals select their own subordinates to be responsible for various state-funded institutions, such as schools and kindergartens. Refusing to take part in such mobilization is essentially out of the question.

---

69 https://meduza.io/feature/2019/09/06/kak-falsifitsirovat-vybory-chtoby-potom-ne-bylo-problem [in Russian].

These supervisors pass down the instructions to state-funded entities, where management appoints staff responsible for ensuring target election numbers. For example, in schools, they require staff to vote in person and bring 3-5 more people by either convincing them or forcing them to come. Every precinct electoral commission has someone in charge of making sure government employees show up to vote; most often these are principals of local schools or heads of municipal enterprises. Before elections, they are given so-called "mobilization lists" with contact information of all workers eligible to vote in the specific voting precinct. Some regions set up municipality-wide databases of government employees who can be mobilized. State employees working in various cities reported being required to go vote, e.g., employees of the Federal Penitentiary Administration, Federal Tax Service, housing and communal services, transportation companies, municipal administration, cultural institutions, and other state-funded organizations. Almost always, they were asked to bring their families to vote, too.

Some of these "quests for voter turnout" created electoral "masterpieces:" for example, in 2020, when voting on amendments to the Constitution, in the Bryansk region town of Klintzy,[70] turnout was 91% in even-numbered precincts, and 90% in odd-numbered precincts, with just a few exceptions. The number of those voting in favor of the Constitutional amendments was expressed in round numbers, with a variance of

---

70 https://kireev.livejournal.com/1761478.html [in Russian].

0.001%. Voter turnout in Bryansk region was much higher than the average in Russia: 86%, and it was the highest in the Central Federal District.

Especially varied is the arsenal of tools used to guarantee a desired election outcome. The regions' task is to attain a target number set by the presidential administration. Regions that fail to produce the desired result are held responsible, and the particular region's governor is probably going to be removed from his post soon as "no longer trustworthy." With every election, the task becomes more complicated – after all, surgical precision is needed in order to show that popular support is as strong as ever and in order to minimize the risk of protest attitudes due to suspicions of falsified results. The target number is 70% or more of voters "showing support."

Elections are mobilization – first of all, mobilization of those who earn their living from the state. State employees play a role in these elections and so do celebrities – in show business, movies, science, or sports. They become agents, or they star in video promos advocating a vote for the ruling party's candidate. Clearly, in a mafia state, cultural figures are an integral part of the mafia state. Among "record holders" is Channel One TV host Leonid Yakubovich who joined the United Russia Party in 2004. In 1996, Yakubovich was Yeltsin's personal representative, and he was Putin's personal representative three times – in 2004, 2012 and 2018. Another mafia state professional "recruit" is actor Mikhail Boyarsky. Boyarsky was Putin's personal representative three times: during the elections of 2004, 2012 and

2018, supporting all initiatives, whether building Gazprom headquarters in St. Petersburg, the annexation of Crimea, or raising the retirement age. He was also a personal representative of the United Russia Party.

Well-known people at the federal or local level are sometimes brought in blatantly to hoodwink voters using a technique called "steamrolling." In such a scenario, a prominent individual who does not really intend to run for office announces his candidacy. After winning, he withdraws, ceding his seat to a lesser-known party member. "Steamrolling" is a favorite technique of the United Russia Party. During the 2003 Duma elections, 38 candidates (37 of whom were from the United Russia Party), withdrew [after winning]. In 2007, the number of such candidates grew to 132 (116 of those from United Russia). United Russia "steamrollers" included a Russian Federation President, heads of 65 regions, three ministers, and several mayors. In 2011, "steamrolling" was used again: 111 candidates elected to the Duma (99 of whom were from United Russia), withdrew after winning. Among United Russia "steamrollers" that year were acting RF President Dmitry Medvedev, heads of 54 regions, and 8 members of the Russian government. During the 2021 State Duma elections, a leader on the United Russia federal list was director of Kommunarka [township] hospital Denis Protsenko, who gained fame during the coronavirus epidemic. After winning the election, he withdrew.

Another method is manipulating the election date. For example, in March 2018, the voting date was moved by a week, thus coinciding with the anniversary of the annexation of Crimea, which enabled those in power to utilize the support of Russians inspired by that event.

Aside from creative new electoral methods, tried-and true, if banal, methods are also used, such as ballot stuffing, “carousels”,[71] rewriting election result tallies, and manipulating absentee ballots. The introduction of an electronic voting system created new ways of controlling elections. On September 8, 2019, Russia conducted an experiment: for the first time, instead of appearing in person at polling stations, citizens could vote using their computers or smart phones. The system was tested in three electoral circuits for the Moscow State Duma elections: the 1st, the 10th and the 30th circuit. In the 30th circuit, electronic voting results were decisive. In traditional voting precincts, self-nominee Roman Yuneman won, but due to “anomalies in electronic voting,” city hall-supported Margarita Rusetskaya was declared winner. And that’s just one example.

Anyone who disagrees with these practices or is barred from running can appeal to the court. Of course, the problem is that the court is part of the same system.

---

71 https://ru.wikipedia.org/wiki/Карусель_(выборы) [in Russian].

Control over the Parliament

"Power is not given, it is won. And after power is won, it's not given up so easily." That's how Sergei Shoigu rather straightforwardly spelled out future goals. Shoigu had agreed to head the *Edinstvo* (Unity) movement created ahead of the 1999 Duma elections. A couple of years later, *Edinstvo* grew into the United Russia Party. Right from the start, the matter thus was of a specific instrument for gaining, utilizing, and retaining power. It seems today as if Putin has always had a Duma majority, but that is not the case – the majority was ultimately won only after initially losing to the Communists.

It all began in mid-August 1999, on the anniversary of the default.[72] Former CIS executive secretary Boris Berezovsky went on a hush-hush tour of Russian regions. Even before he left, rumors circulated that Berezovsky was trying to put together a new gubernatorial bloc that would become a political force acting in the Kremlin's interests. The summer of 1999 was not easy for Yeltsin, the Family [his inner circle], and the presidential administration. Merely six months

---

72 A reference to the serious economic crisis in Russia of 17 August 1998 when Prime Minister Sergei Kirienko announced a series of economic measures that, in fact, constituted a default and devaluation of the ruble.

remained until Duma elections, and the *Otechestvo-Vsya Rossiya* (Fatherland – All Russia) political bloc headed by Moscow Mayor Yuri Luzhkov, former prime minister Evgeny Primakov, and Tatarstan head Mentimer Shaimiev was becoming the most popular force in the country. So popular, that many, even some of the elite, saw Luzhkov and Primakov as Yeltsin's successors and future Russian rulers.

Yeltsin's daughter Tatyana Dyachenko later said that Berezovsky was full of new, often extravagant ideas. She wrote in her blog: "Before the 1999 parliamentary elections, another idea fired his imagination: creating a new party that would enter the parliament. Berezovsky did not have either a name for the party or an understanding of what kind of party this would be; he simply had an idea. He believed that a new leader, a presidential candidate, needs his own party, a new party that people would not associate with any old, pro-government parties, such as *Nash Dom – Rossiya* (Our Home is Russia), *Demokratichesky Vybor Rossii* (Russia's Democratic Choice), etc. I clearly recall the first discussions regarding this at presidential administration head Aleksandr Voloshin's *dacha*, where Berezovsky ardently, noisily, and emotionally declared that a future president can't do without his own party, that every president must have his own party. And Yeltsin made a serious mistake by failing to create his own party on which he could rely."[73]

---

73 https://obshchayagazeta.eu/news/2010/02/08/47114?ysclid=lkv0kekpk515325893 [in Russian].

Now the task was bringing to power a person who was not at all a politician. A political support structure had to be set up quickly.

In late September, just three months before the election, the formation of Edinstvo was announced. They were counting on administrative resources. Governors known for their highly authoritarian leadership style formed the backbone: Evgeny Nazdratenko (Primorye), Leonid Gorbenko (Kaliningrad region), Nikolai Kondratenko (Krasnodar Krai), and Aleksandr Rutskoy (Kursk region). In their electoral precincts, overwhelming votes for this bloc had to be secured. *Edinstvo* leaders were the popular Ministry of Emergency Situations head Sergei Shoigu, the equally popular wrestler Aleksandr Karelin, and Aleksandr Gurov, who at the time headed the Ministry of Internal Affairs Institute.

Less than a month before the elections, Putin announced that he supported *Edinstvo* and would vote for it. By his own admission, as then-prime minister, Putin wasn't supposed to "specify his political leanings" with regard to pre-election blocs, but as a citizen and Sergei Shoigu's friend he simply had to react to the bloc's promise to "support the current government."

After Putin's statement, *Edinstvo's* ratings almost doubled, according to polls. This was not enough, however, to win the election. The bloc received 23.32% of the votes, losing to the Communists, who received 24.29%, but surpassing *Otechestvo-Vsya Rossiya* (OVR), which received 13.33%. Nevertheless, this movement took second place in parliament's lower chamber despite having no history, no ideology, and no specific platform. This was due to the administrative resources and to the Berezovsky-controlled media, primarily TV, which was also used intensely to attack opponents.

After Putin was elected president, it was clear that the OVR leadership could no longer operate independently; they had to fall in line with Putin's system, which was looking to expand and to create a centrist coalition as a counterweight to the RF Communist Party. Putin needed a manageable Duma with no potential risk of it's becoming a source of conflict for the president. The bargaining and negotiations lasted almost a year, culminating on December 1, 2001, when *Edinstvo*, *Otechestvo* and *Vsya Rossiya* announced that they will join to form the *Edinaya Rossiya* (United Russia) Party (which had been preceded by the alliance *Edinstvo i Otechestvo*" (Unity and Fatherland), a political union headed by Shoigu, Luzhkov and Shaimiev.

As a result of the 2003 and 2011 elections, United Russia had a majority in the State Duma, and in 2007 and 2016 – a supermajority. At the same time, few would call United Russia a ruling party. Grigory Golosov more accurately describes United Russia's role: it's not a ruling party, it's an *electoral instrument used by the executive power in order to control the State Duma*. This instrument frequently proved useful.

Simultaneously, the upper chamber of the Parliament, the Federation Council, also became subordinate after undergoing a Putin-initiated internal reform. Governors and heads of local legislative bodies in the Federation Council were replaced with appointed permanent representatives, with one representative appointed by the regional governor, and the other one – "by the region's legislative body."

Establishing control over the Parliament guaranteed unimpeded adoption of laws in the mafia group's interests. An additional bonus – no public discussion of hot-button issues at the parliamentary level. In 2003, parliament speaker Boris Gryzlov quite accurately described a parliament's job in a mafia state: "I don't think the State Duma is a platform for conducting political battles or defending some political slogans and ideologies – it is a platform for engaging in constructive, effective legislative activity." The famous tenet – "Parliament is not a place for discussions."

All this came in very handy during what the Russians call a "special operation." The speed with which laws were being adopted amazed not only observers but also some participants in the process. For example, in April 2023, the State Duma adopted the law on electronic military draft notices and a unified register of reservists at lightning speed: members [elsewhere we say "members," as does the Duma's own website in English; I prefer "members"] voted on the measure essentially without ever having read the text of the bill, which was published just hours before the State Duma adopted the law in all three readings. RF Communist Party faction Parliament member Nina Ostanina noted: "I don't recall an entire law being passed after a TV interview, with just two hours in the room to review the law." No matter –

the law passed unanimously, with one person abstaining, and even he later said that it had been a mistake.

The monopolization of power is best illustrated by the composition of the 7th session of the State Duma elected in 2016.

Faction	Number of Duma members	Expressed in %
United Russia	341	76.12%
RF Communist Party	42	9.38%
LDPR	40	8.93%
Just Russia	23	5.13%
Unaffiliated Duma members	2	0.45%

Ensuring the Power Vertical

On September 28, 2010, at 8:00 am, President Dmitry Medvedev published a decree on removing Moscow Mayor Yuri Luzhkov from his post due to a "loss of trust." A few days earlier, Luzhkov, upon returning from his vacation, had announced that he had no plans to resign despite the large-scale media attack against him and his wife Elena Baturina. Later, in his memoirs, Luzhkov noted: "Strange as it seems, in democratic Russia, my removal took place in accordance with the well-known old Soviet scenario: In order to remove a leader who has fallen out of favor, "criticism by the Party" would be published in the Party Central Committee's *Pravda* newspaper, or in the USSR Supreme Soviet's *Izvestiya* newspaper, after which he was removed from his post."

Luzhkov, who was one of United Russia's founders, was popular with the people and had a decent relationship with Putin. Luzhkov didn't see Medvedev as a real president, and he underestimated him. The conflict between Luzhkov and Medvedev slowly brewed, and became public when Luzhkov's article was published in state-run *Rossiiskaya Gazeta*,[74] which stated, among other things: "There is a very somber public mood right now that's not in line with developmental tasks." Fol-

74 https://rg.ru/2010/09/06/mer.html?ysclid=lh31y-9oe1133235408 [in Russian].

lowing the article, Medvedev suggested that all government officials "either take part in improving public institutions, or join the opposition."

Luzhkov persisted, and Medvedev chose a hardline way to end the conflict with the hard-hitting mayor. By removing Luzhkov, Medvedev not only proved that he was indeed president, but he also fulfilled Putin's wish of subordinating governors, stripping them of the vestiges of their autonomy. In a letter to Medvedev, Luzhkov wrote: "You need another Moscow mayor, one of your own. Luzhkov is independent and inconvenient."[75] Of course this is very subjective, but it also rings true. You can't be part of the system and play by your own rules at the same time. Putin's silence showed that Luzhkov never became an insider, and, unlike Shoigu, never joined the narrow *mafiosi* circle. Luzhkov thus could be removed in the interests of the entire system, in accordance with the wishes of one of the system's top members – Medvedev.

Bashkortostan head Murtaza Rakhimov was removed before Luzhkov, although less harshly: he agreed to voluntarily resign before the end of his term. Medvedev continued the policies that Putin had started regarding region heads. Almost immediately after taking power, Vladimir Putin started stripping governors of power at the federal level. The Federation Council was the subject of one of the first reforms: governors were

---

75 https://www.vedomosti.ru/politics/articles/2010/09/29/luzhkov_obvinil_medvedeva_v_profanacii_demokratii?ysclid=lkv10rb26u622292682 [in Russian].

replaced by regional representatives coordinated with the center. Governors thus lost the ability to develop ties and to lobby for regional interests centrally. Moreover, the 1999 elections had shown that united governors are a force to be reckoned with, capable of affecting policies in the country; it was important to prevent unsanctioned alliances. The fear that regions and local elites might become independent was a complex that remained from the collapse of the USSR.

During the next stage, governors were stripped of political independence; they were subordinated to the power vertical and now reported to the center. This happened in 2004, when a law was passed abolishing elections of heads of subjects of the Federation. Now, they had to be approved by local legislative bodies, according to the president's nomination. Putin personally initiated the abolition of such elections. Since then, governors became directly politically dependent on the Kremlin. In 2012, direct gubernatorial elections were reinstated, but, as experts noted, in conditions of electoral authoritarianism, gubernatorial elections are "successful," and the Kremlin's candidates confidently win. Electoral techniques run smoothly: the system of municipal filters blocks strong opponents; low voter turnout guarantees the necessary outcome.[76] There were some "malfunctions" here and there, as, for instance, when residents voted for someone – anyone – other than the government-supported candidate, but

---

76 https://openuni.io/course/11-course-7-4/lesson/6/material/875/ [in Russian].

the well-oiled system made it possible to subordinate or remove even those election winners, as was done, for example, with Khabarovsk Krai governor Sergei Furgal.

Moreover, regions are very dependent financially on the federal center. Regional budgets' income derives from regional taxes (organizations' property taxes, transport), federal tax and levy allocations to the RF subjects, and various grants, subsidies, and transfer payments from the federal budget. Every year, 72-73 regions receive grants.

The most sought-after and easily collected tax income goes to the federal budget, not regional budgets.

Restructuring regional management radically changed the regional leaderships' goals and tasks. The objective of fighting for your region's interests in Moscow or accountability to the population that you represent became secondary. *The regional leadership's main task now became implementing the mafia clan's policies at the local level, and maintaining loyalty.* Equally important, regional leaders must not stand in the way of their regions becoming a "feeding trough" for federal groups inside the mafia clan.

Unsurprisingly, under Putin, the practice of appointing "Vikings" (outsiders) to gubernatorial posts became widespread. For example, Kaliningrad Region governor Anton Alikhanov, born in 1986, never had any connection to that region – he was simply making a federal bureaucratic career. Similarly, Lipetsk governor Igor Artamonov was always far removed from Lipetsk. Same with Nizhny Novgorod region governor Gleb Nikitin.

Their interests are focused on the center; their future career depends on Moscow, where they hope at some point to obtain a federal position . Such governors sent to the regions acquired the name *"Putin's technocrats," which quite accurately describes the technical, rather than political, nature of the post, the lack of personal ambitions outside the system, and the overarching loyalty*. Other than technocrats, governor appointees were *siloviki*, primarily from the Federal Protection Service and the FSB. Some examples are Tula Region governor Aleksei Dyumin, Astrakhan Region governor Igor Babushkin, and Yaroslav Region governor Dmitry Mironov. The population sees both types as "Vikings" who have no knowledge of the region's particular features, no emotional ties to the region, and no desire to understand or take into account the residents' needs.

Increasingly, as the power vertical is solidified, governors more and more are becoming coordinators responsible for implementing instructions from above. The appointment model that used to frighten the regions' political elites actually became a salvation for many of them and allowed them to keep their power for three terms and beyond. The Kremlin's substitutes' bench turned out to be rather short, and the federal elites were not prepared to put political stability in the regions at risk.[77]

Moscow's desires regarding the regions are fairly simple: political stability, ensuring voter turnouts and desired results, and no regional revolts, especially the

---

77 http://rossovmir.ru/files/_1_2009.pdf [in Russian].

kind that spread outside the region and gain significance on a federal level. After the full-scale invasion of Ukraine, additional responsibilities entailed assembling, organizing, and equipping those called to active duty.

Some regions achieve outstanding results. Standouts here are "electoral sultanates," marked by unusually high voter turnout and the proportion of votes cast for the party in power. Some examples include several North Caucasus regions (in particular, Chechnya and Dagestan), Bashkortostan, Mordovia, Tatarstan, Tyva, Kuzbas, Tyumen Region, and Yamal-Nenets Autonomous Region.[78] Special characteristics of governance, the use of administrative resources, elites' interaction, and the lack of independent election monitoring all produce a decent result. It is noteworthy that Dagestan, Ingushetia, Chechnya, and Tyva are regions where federal grants are a main income source.[79]

At the same time, a multi-tiered system of control over the regions and local governments was put in place: local *siloviki*, who are subordinate to the Moscow leadership, the president's authorized representatives in federal districts, state companies located in various parts of the country that naturally are able to influence the population (especially in one-factory towns and towns where the company is the main employer) and to control local governments, both by appointing their

---

78 https://www.rbc.ru/politics/22/03/2018/5ab0e12b9a79477b98c164cb [in Russian].

79 https://newtimes.ru/articles/detail/116599 [in Russian].

own people to positions and through financial support of the towns and regions. In addition, there are federal ministries and various kinds of "supervisory bodies," as well as the All-Russia People's Front that keeps track of fluctuations of stability and loyalty.

There is a minimal but effective arsenal on hand to handle those who became undesirable: either voluntary resignation or removal through criminal prosecution or due to loss of trust. The most frequently used weapon against regional elites is a charge of corruption. Such accusations have nothing to do with actually fighting corruption – it's merely a matter of removing unwanted local representatives.

Between 2000 and 2020, thirty acting or former governors were criminally prosecuted,[80] most notably former LDPR State Duma deputy Sergei Furgal, who became head of Khabarovsk territory [*krai*]. The arrest of "the people's governor" evoked a massive protest in the region, unseen in other regions. Furgal had been elected in September 2018, as a form of protest by Khabarovsk residents against United Russia and its appointee, acting governor Vyacheslav Shport. Furgal did not conduct an active election campaign, but he made it to the second round of elections and defeated Shport, gathering 69.6% of votes. Furgal refused to withdraw from the race before the second round. After Vyacheslav Shport lost, the Kremlin symbolically exacted

---

80 https://novayagazeta.ru/articles/2020/07/10/86230-vzyatochnik-tipichney-krovopiytsy?ysclid=lh34cu7x-pk988418949 [in Russian].

revenge on the entire region by moving the capital of the Far East District from Khabarovsk to Vladivostok.

Furgal became a symbol of opposition to Moscow, the Kremlin, and United Russia. What's worse, as Furgal's ratings grew, Vladimir Putin's ratings in the region dropped. After the 2019 election to the legislative assembly, Khabarovsk territory became the first region where LDPR, and not United Russia, attained a constitutional majority.

In the end, Furgal, in essence, followed Luzhkov's path, with the only difference that he was a total outsider to the system, which is why much harsher measures were taken against him than against Luzhkov. In summer 2020, he was arrested on charges of organizing murders and an attempted murder allegedly committed in 2004-2005. At the time, Vladimir Zhirinovsky quite logically commented on Furgal's arrest by the regime: "Why were you silent for 14 years? For 15 years you said nothing? He ran for Khabarovsk krai Duma – you were silent; he was State Duma deputy three times – you said nothing. Now that he's running for governor – be quiet!" Zhirinovsky also identified the main reason his colleague fell out of favor: Sergei Furgal was approached many times by former Khabarovsk krai governor Vyacheslav Shport's former chief of staff, who asked Furgal to take "a small crate (of money) to Moscow." "They tell him the amount; they say they take it there every year. And it's like that all over the country! For three years, he refused, he didn't deliver three boxes to Moscow! And that's it!" Zhirinovsky said, in essence exposing the corrupt chain of Putin's hierarchy in which "tributes" from the regions are sent to Moscow.

The regional governance system is essentially a copy of the federal system and subject to the same vices: the propensity for nepotism, appointing "one's own people," including relatives and trusted individuals, even if they are not professionals. In the regions, the governors control all financial flows and force businesses to take the governors' interests into account.

A vivid example of this is Chechnya, where Ramzan Kadyrov (who essentially inherited power) appoints his children, sisters, in-laws, nephews, and various cousins to government positions. In 2018, the BBC Russian Service published an investigation asserting that, of 158 Chechen officials, around one-third had family ties with Kadyrov.[81]

Federally appointed "Viking" governors also bring their colleagues, acquaintances and even relatives to the regions. For example, in 2008, former Yakutsk mayor Ilya Mikhalchuk became Archangelsk region governor, after which his fellow countrymen took all the key posts in the regional administration: Mikhalchuk's son became head of United Russia's executive committee, his stepsister (who had been prosecuted for improprieties in real estate) became head of the regional property department, his wife's nephew became deputy mayor of Arkhangelsk for construction matters and was soon accused of corruption. In 2012, he voluntarily resigned. Before that, President Medvedev harshly criticized him

---

81 https://www.kavkazr.com/a/klan-kadyrovyh-polnyy-spisok-rodstvennikov-glavy-chechni-vo-vlasti/32066496.html [in Russian].

due to numerous scandals in the region's housing sector after a report by an authorized representative to the Northwestern Federal District.

PURGING THE MEDIA

The media are often called the "fourth estate." A mafia state cannot permit any power other than itself; it therefore destroys anything it does not control – civil society organizations and independent media. To do this, the mafia state has a wide assortment of tools, which are, according to Magyar: *nationalization – absorption – subjugation – taming – isolating in a "ghetto" – dislodging – elimination*. All of these were used against the media in Russia starting in 2000 throughout Vladimir Putin's rule. Independent media were either crushed and shut down, or they were taken over by either the government or by industrial groups close to the Kremlin. Another option was that people loyal to the government were installed to head the media outlets' editorial boards. Some media outlets were able to relocate, with entire editorial offices leaving Russia (especially after February 2022) and continuing to operate from abroad. The Russian media was controlled using legislative restrictions, judicial or financial pressure, criminal prosecution, or outright takeover. At the same time, a powerful propaganda machine was put in place, with an operating budget of billions in state funds.

Putin, whose presidency would not have been possible without media manipulation, views the media as a weapon, not as an instrument to serve the public interest. And only people Putin personally selects and controls are allowed to have this weapon. This, incidentally, is different from Soviet totalitarianism. In the USSR, all media outlets were owned and controlled by the government, but in a mafia state, both the government and members of the mafia group can take charge of the media on an equal basis, creating a hybrid media space of sorts. This situation allows even private media to exist, as long as the owners are subordinated to the system and play by its rules. All other, truly independent media outlets are subjected to pressure, persecution, and repression. This affects entire publications as well as individual journalists. An environment is created that makes it impossible for media to function outside of centralized control.

How did this happen? It all started with television, which was the main tool for influencing people's minds, especially in the early 2000s.

When Vladimir Putin came to power in Russia in 2000, five large federal TV channels were broadcasting informational programs: ORT, RTR, NTV, TV-6 and REN TV. The mouthpiece of the official government agenda was the state-owned RTR channel (later renamed *Rossiya-1*) owned by the All-Russian State Television and Radio Broadcasting Company. Other channels conducted their own informational policy, although not for long. NTV and ORT were the first victims. NTV owner (through *Media Most* [Media Bridge]) Vladimir Gusinsky, who was charged with fraud, left Russia, with Gazprom eventually becoming owner of the NTV channel. Gazprom had held 30% of NTV shares since 1996, and *Media Most* owed Gazprom $2,116,000. After the ownership change, the debt was restructured and the cases against Gusinsky were closed. Gradually, NTV became subject to censorship, and Vladimir Solovyev started broadcasting his show *Voskresny Vecher* (Sunday Evening). NTV became an instrument of official and semi-official propaganda. In particular, NTV aired films commissioned by *siloviki* (primarily the FSB) aimed against the Russian opposition (e.g., *The Anatomy of a Protest*), against NGOs (films against the *Golos*[82] [Voice] Association), and against independent businesspeople (a series of films against Yukos shareholders).

Russian Public Television (ORT), which under Putin became Channel One, was created on the initiative of The Association of Independent Television Producers that consisted of VID, ATV and *Klass* TV companies. The state held a controlling share package (51%) through *Ostankino* Russian Public TV and Radio Company. Ideology, however, was mainly determined by Boris Berezovsky (whose LogoVAZ held 8% of ORT) and by Berezovsky's people working for the channel.

In September 2000, Berezovsky published an open letter to President Putin in *Kommersant*, which read: "Last week, a high-ranking official from your administration gave me an ultimatum: turn over my shares in ORT to the state, or follow Gusinsky, apparently meaning Butyrka prison. The reason for such a proposal is your dissatisfaction over how ORT reported on events related to the Kursk submarine accident. 'The President wants to run ORT himself,' your representative told me.

---

82 An organization founded in 2000 to monitor elections in Russia.

After Gusinsky was essentially exiled from the country and Gazprom (read: the state) took control over NTV, ORT is the only nationwide channel that is not totally dependent on the state. If I accept the ultimatum, then televised information in Russia will end and will be replaced with televised propaganda controlled by your advisors."[83]

That is exactly what happened. Berezovsky emigrated, and ORT became one of the main state propaganda tools. The only one who remained was Konstantin Ernst, who not only adapted to the new reality, but even began to shape it. By early 2001, it became known that Berezovsky sold 49% of ORT shares to oligarch Roman Abramovich (with the state retaining the controlling interest), and the board of directors was now manned almost exclusively by government representatives or people close to it. You could forget all about the public interest at this point. Starting September 2, 2002, ORT was renamed Channel One JSC (Joint-Stock Company). In early 2011, billionaire businessman Yuri Kovalchuk's *Natsionalnaya Media Gruppa* (National Media Group – NMG) bought 25% of Channel One shares from Abramovich's companies. Abramovich later sold all his shares, while NMG absorbed another independent TV channel, REN TV. It is worth noting that Yuri Kovalchuk does not simply hold media assets on behalf of the mafia group: *Proekt* (Project), an investigative journalism media outlet called him the second most-influ-

---

83 https://www.kommersant.ru/doc/157013? [in Russian].

ential person in the nation.[84] Russian domestic policy and propaganda content largely depend on Kovalchuk's views and how he presents his views to Putin as Putin's closest friend and confidant.

Berezovsky's second TV project – Channel TV-6, where many of the journalists who left NTV worked, including Evgeny Kiselev, was simply shut down. This occurred on the initiative of *Lukoil-Garant* pension fund that was part of Lukoil Oil Company, which held 15% of *TV-6 Moskva* shares. Similar processes were occurring on the regional level, too. For example, in early 2015, Tomsk TV-2 Channel ceased operations; its editor-in-chief Viktor Muchnik said the reason for its shut-down was the authorities' inability to influence TV-2's editorial policy.

It is insufficient for the mafia state to have total control over media outlets broadcasting to the Russian audience. The mafia state's interests (financial, ideological, political) are much broader. On June 6, 2005, it was announced that a new TV channel called Russia Today would start operating in the fall, designed to "reflect Russia's position on main international policy issues" and "inform the audience about events and developments in Russian life." The new channel was the brainchild of Mikhail Lesin and was founded by state-owned *RIA Novosti* (Russian Information Agency News) through its subsidiary *TV-Novosti*. Journalist Margarita Simonyan was appointed editor-in-chief. The channel was to become an official Russian propaganda tool directed at the foreign audience.

---

84 https://maski-proekt.media/yury-kovalchuk/ [in Russian].

RT (Russia Today) is funded by the state, and its budget grew exponentially over the years: In 2007, the channel received 2.4 billion rubles and 10 years later it reached 18.74 billion rubles.

There were also legislative attacks on independent media. For example, on October 15, 2014, Vladimir Putin signed a law limiting foreign ownership of Russian media.[85] According to this law, foreign holdings of any Russian media outlet may not exceed 20% (the limit was formerly 50% and did not extend to print and internet publications). When the new rule took effect on January 1, 2016, foreign owners of Russian media outlets had either to sell their assets or give a significant part thereof to local partners. At the time, the Russian media market was represented by three main media types: state media, private Russian media, and private media with foreign capital or published under foreign media licenses. Under the old law, the media with Western capital and licensed media were the least vulnerable to Russian governmental influence on editorial policy.

A massive redistribution took place in the media market, with new owners taking over TV channels, individual media projects, and publishing houses. Many of these new owners were close to the mafia clan.

Starting in 2000, over 130 bills related to regulating the media were introduced in the State Duma: gradually, the authorities increased the media's liability for extremism, violations of electoral law, and disclosing

---

85 https://www.rbc.ru/society/15/10/2014/543e1d69cbb20fef76d559f7 [in Russian].

personal data.[86] The most significant legislative restrictions in this sphere started after the 2011–2012 protests and peaked after the February 2022 full-scale invasion of Ukraine.

After 2011, print and online media outlets found themselves under massive pressure: crackdowns on editorial offices, shutting down of websites, obstructing operations. For example, *Kommersant-Vlast'* weekly's longtime editor-in-chief Maksim Kovalsky was fired from *Kommersant* Publishing House for publishing a photograph of a ballot with a profanity written next to Vladimir Putin's name. Later, media manager Demyan Kudryavtsev left *Kommersant* Publishing House. In 2016, Vladimir Zhelonkin, who previously headed the *Zvezda* (Star) media group became *Kommersant* Publishing House's general manager.[87] In 2019, *Kommersant* newspaper wrote that Federation Council chairperson Valentina Matvienko might be going to work at the Russian Pension Fund. The Publishing House owner Alisher Usmanov objected to the article and fired its authors. In a show of solidarity, all political department journalists, as well as deputy editor-in-chief Gleb Cherkasov also resigned.

Shortly before the 2011 Duma elections, Roman Badanin resigned as editor-in-chief of one of the largest online publications in Russia, *Gazeta.ru*, because management decided to remove from the website a banner of

---

86 https://www.kommersant.ru/doc/2733613 [in Russian].

87 https://meduza.io/feature/2016/05/17/12-redaktsiy-za-pyat-let [in Russian].

a joint project with the *Golos* human rights organization. As part of that project, readers submitted reports of violations committed during the election campaign. After the 2012 elections, Aleksandr Mamut took over SUP Media holding company that owned *Gazeta.ru*.

In December 2013, by Vladimir Putin's decree, *RIA Novosti* state information agency was disbanded, and a new agency formed instead, called *MIA Rossiya Segodnya* (Russia Today International News Agency), with the main Russian tele-propagandist Dmitry Kiselev appointed general manager and RT TV head Margarita Simonyan appointed editor-in-chief.

In 2014, the *Grani.ru* website was blocked by the General Prosecutor's Office's order on the grounds that it allegedly incited illegal activity and participation in unlawful mass gatherings. *Grani.ru* was the first website to be blocked in Russia; the same day, the Federal Service for Supervision of Communications, Information Technology, and Mass Media [*Roskomnadzor*] demanded that access to the sites *Kasparov.ru*[88] and *EZH.ru* [Ezhednevny zhurnal (Daily Journal)] be restricted on the same grounds.

The Foreign Agents Law of 2021 became the main weapon against independent media projects and individual journalists – primarily, those involved in investigative journalism. *Dozhd'* [Rain] TV channel and the publications *Meduza*, *Vtimes* (founded by former *Vedomosti* staff), *The Insider*, *The Bell*, and dozens of individ-

---

88 Site run by Putin opponent, former chess champion Garry Kasparov.

ual journalists were declared "foreign agents," which meant that they had to indicate that whatever content they published was "created by a foreign agent." Some projects were branded "undesirable organizations," as was, for example, *Meduza* and an outlet called *Project.* Mikhail Khodorkovsky shut down his media projects Open Media and MBK Media due to the risks of criminal prosecution for collaborating with an undesirable organization.

While Putin's people were attacking TV stations, newspapers, and journals, the Russian people turned to the internet. According to *Mediascope* analytical group, by early 2010, an average of 75% of Russia's urbanites logged on to the web, while 70.4% watched TV. This means that, on a daily basis, the internet reached a wider audience in Russia than TV,[89] and, to some extent, the web is still a free space, although this freedom is continuously narrowed by the government, sometimes comically. The standoff between the messaging service app *Telegram* and supervisory *Roskomnadzor* was epic. *Telegram* is an oasis for both open-author and anonymous-author channels with audiences ranging from tens of thousands to over a million subscribers.

On July 1, 2017, a law called "Yarovaya's Law" took effect in Russia. The law obligates telecommunications operators to keep records of their customers' phone messages and internet traffic for six months, maintain keys to decrypt users' communication, and provide the

---

89 https://www.vedomosti.ru/technology/articles/2019/05/29/802699-internet-dogonyaet [in Russian].

keys to the FSB on request. *Telegram* refused to give security and intelligence agencies the decrypting keys. In April 2018, *Roskomnadzor* started blocking *Telegram's* IP addresses, blocking over 18 million addresses in the first week. Nevertheless, *Telegram* continued to operate, and it was accessible in Russia the entire time that it was blocked. However, due to *Roskomnadzor*'s actions, other servers suffered: for example, the websites of Skolkovo Institute of Science and Technology, Moscow State University, The Higher School of Economics, the Russian Foundation for Basic Research application systems, among many others. *Roskomnadzor* gave up. But *Telegram* is unusual in fighting for the independence of Russian media: most political channels are controlled by the presidential administration and staffed by propagandists such as Vladimir Solovyev, whereas independent and oppositional channels face pressure from *siloviki* and face administrators' anonymity being lifted. That is how one of the largest channels, Futlyar ot violoncheli (Cello Case) was shut down. After February 2022, *Telegram* played a special role in that it allowed military correspondents to report news from the front lines from the Russian side, with hundreds of thousands of subscribers to the military correspondents' reports, and the military correspondents' influence now equals that of the media.

Unlike Telegram founder Pavel Durov, who is located outside of Russia, Yandex founders (Yandex is one of the largest Russian internet servers) had a large portion of their business inside Russia, which meant it was impossible to escape the mafia group's control. The mafia group was interested in Yandex for two reasons: one was control, censorship, and propaganda, and the other one was income from this profitable large business. Therefore, for starters, a "gold share" was issued and "sold" for a symbolic one Euro to Sberbank, which enabled Sberbank to block some deals, including sale of more than 25% of Yandex shares. This was insufficient, however, and pressure on Yandex continued for years. In the mafia state there was no doubt that, in case of refusal, Yandex would be destroyed. In summer 2019, a bill was introduced into the State Duma known as "Duma Deputy Gorelkin's Law." The bill proposed that foreigners should not be allowed to hold more than 20% of shares in Russian companies that have "significant informational resources for developing an informational and communications infrastructure in the RF, as well as data processing technology." The day after the bill was publicly discussed, Yandex' stock prices plummeted by 15%. In November 2019, Yandex unveiled a new ownership and management structure that looked like the lesser of two evils as compared to Gorelkin's proposal. The draft proposal was coordinated with the presidential administration and government officials. The mediator between the state and the Yandex leadership was Aleksandr Voloshin, former presidential administration head and chairman of the board of directors of Yandex . The main innovation was creating an NGO, the Public Interest Foundation and Sberbank's transferring Yandex's "golden share" to the new Foundation. Under the new management setup, Yandex must coordinate with the Foundation if consolidating 10% or more of Yandex shares or transmitting significant intellectual property or users' personal data. The Foundation also got the right temporarily to remove Yandex' general manager in Russia. Duma deputy Gorelkin then withdrew his bill, and the corresponding law was passed in the government's less bloodthirsty version.

Nevertheless, Yandex suffered a sad fate. Its demise was pre-determined by its very attempt to find a compromise with the mafia state. After Russia invaded Ukraine, Tigran Khudaverdyan, chief managing director of the parent company Yandex N.V. became the subject of EU sanctions, after which the EU imposed sanctions on Arkady Volozh. One of the grounds cited was that Yandex promoted government media and removed content that criticized the Russian government.

In December 2022, Volozh left Yandex. Before that, a deal was struck transferring the entire media component to individuals serving state interests. *Dzen* and *Novosti* services were sold to VK [Vkontakte, online Russian networking service] headed by Vladimir Kirienko (Sergei Kirienko's son), while Yandex received *Delivery Club* Service, formerly owned by VK.

On 5 February 2024, Dutch Yandex N.V. announced the sale of its Russian business for 475 billion rubles to a consortium of Russian investors. The management company FMP will buy 35% of the Russian shares of Yandex; in addition, Lukoil, former chairman of the board of Gazprom Aleksandr Ryazanov, and a couple of other people are supposed to become joint holders.

"Special operation" mode and the rout of the media

The Russian media probably never before experienced such a crushing rout as it did in February 2022 – unless you count the closure of "bourgeois" (non-Soviet) and oppositional newspapers in 1917-1918. In early March 2022, shortly after the full-scale invasion, a law was passed in Russia that the people labeled "for fakes about the special op," which provides for punishment of up to 15 years in jail. Articles were added to the Code of Administrative Offences and the Criminal Code that made it a crime to discredit the armed forces, with perpetrators subject to incarceration.

The Criminal Code was amended on March 6, and, by March 8, *Agora* International Group lawyers and *OVD-Info* Human Rights Project documented at least 144 prosecutions under the new article for discrediting the Russian armed forces (AVC Art. 20.3.3.). Most of those prosecuted were anti-war protesters, and "evidence" of breaking the law were banners the protesters were holding, such as "No to War" and "Peace on Earth."[90]

But even before this latest law passed, *Roskomnadzor* notified the following media outlets that they must restrict access to "false information": *Echo Moskvy* (Echo of Moscow), *InoSMI* (Foreign media),

---

90 https://www.kommersant.ru/doc/5249929 [in Russian].

Svobodnaya Pressa (Free Press), *Novaya Gazeta* (The New Newspaper), *Lenizdat*, New Times, as well as media outlets labeled as "foreign agents" in Russia: Dozhd' (Rain) TV channel, *Mediazona* (Media Zone) and Krym.Realii (Crimea Realities). The notice from the supervisory federal agency read: "The indicated resources published, under the guise of being true, false information of public significance regarding shelling of Ukrainian cities and deaths of Ukrainian civilians as a result of Russian armed forces' operations, and also materials describing the ongoing operation as an attack, invasion, or declaration of war." Thus, it became illegal in Russia to use the word "war" to describe the Russian forces' full-scale invasion of Ukraine, and it also became illegal to call for peace or an end to the war. Pacifism became illegal. Just as in Orwell's book *1984*: war is peace, freedom is slavery, ignorance is strength.

After warnings from *Roskomnadzor* and the risk of criminal prosecution, Russian media outlets whose position may have been perceived as differing from the official position suspended or ceased operations in rapid succession. *Dozhd* TV channel announced that it was suspending operations, and Ekho Moskvy's board of directors decided to shut down both the radio station, which had been operating since 1990, and its website. The longest holdout was *Novaya Gazeta*, but even it announced on March 28, 2022 that it would suspend its publication until the "special operation in Ukraine" ends. A while later, however, many editorial offices were able to relocate and continue working from abroad.

Culture and the arts in the service of the mafia state

In a 2012 election video, a young woman with sad eyes says on-camera: "Nothing in our life is more precious than children's health. Vladimir Putin has never been indifferent to requests from the *Podari Zhizn'* (The Gift of Life) Foundation or from doctors the foundation supports. Vladimir Putin always fulfilled his promises to The Gift of Life. Help must be tangible. That's why I'll be voting for him." Chulpan Khamatova is an actress at Moscow's *Sovremennik* theater and a founder of the Gift of Life Foundation. The video's goal was to ensure state support for the foundation's projects that help children with oncological and hematological diseases. Of course, no one applies direct pressure, and no one says outright: "If you don't ensure voter turnout, children won't be helped." But the rules of the game are clear by default: as a protégé of the state, in exchange for its loyalty, the foundation will have more administrative opportunities than it would have had without closeness to the president.

In an interview a few years later, Khamatova explained everything in a rather straightforward way: "First of all, I really was grateful. Second, I understood back then that the Rogachev Clinic construction had not been completed yet, it was not operating yet. Our doctors who established it – it was their project – were under threat. It was such a tasty morsel. You have no idea how much money could be made from something like oncology, and we have examples, lots of them. There was a hungry swarm around us eager to take the clinic from us. The foundation needs a good relationship, you have to be able to make deals, because there are still many unresolved issues, including the legislative basis. We have to have a dialogue. And I understand that this is my job, my responsibility. Yes, I realized there would be a fallout, but I didn't realize to what extent."[91]

This, case however, was probably an exception in which children's lives and health were involved. Most often it is a lot more banal. Performances (and thus fees as well), titles, and jobs are granted in exchange for serving the regime. Otherwise, as in the case of musician Yuri Shevchuk, who spoke out against the war, it's a dialogue akin to, "Who are you?" – "I am Yura, a musician," and then no more concerts.[92] It's easiest of all with musicians: it's enough merely to bar access to concert venues. A petition by Russian musicians demanding an end to pressure on musicians reads: "Those of us who dared to speak our minds are pressured from every direction. We are bullied by *siloviki*, our concerts turn into police raids, local officials call nightclubs and urge them not to deal with us. Well-known musicians' tours were disrupted, and they do whatever they want

---

91 https://www.kino-teatr.ru/lifestyle/news/y2019/6-20/18407/.

92 https://www.themoscowtimes.com/2022/05/19/soviet-rock-star-prosecuted-for-putins-ass-anti-war-speech-a77732.

with lesser-known musicians."[93] Among the petition's authors were rapper Noize MC, the band *Nogu Svelo* (Leg Cramp), and Aleksei Kortnev (*Neschastny sluchai* [Accident]). After musician Andrei Makarevich spoke out against the war, his band *Mashina Vremeni's* (Time Machine) anniversary concerts were cancelled Russia-wide. The same fate befell the band *Nochnye snaipery* (Night snipers), Valery Meladze, and others. Concerts by all musicians who spoke out against the war were canceled.

The threat of various sorts of crackdowns loomed over cultural figures expressing their anti-war views: for example, actor Dmitry Nazarov was fired from the Chekhov Moscow Art Theater, and Liya Akhejakova was forced to leave *Sovremennik*; Andrei Makarevich and Maksim Galkin were branded "foreign agents;" rapper "Oxxxymiron" was charged with distributing extremist materials; Alla Pugacheva and Liya Akhejakova were slammed in the media.

For many cultural figures, however, regularly showing loyalty to the state is a norm of existence. They are part of the mafia state. They shape the mafia state's culture, sometimes representing a true "hybrid of mafia and [the honorary title] People's Artist." An excellent

---

93 https://www.change.org/p/администрация-президента-рф-требуем-прекратить-давление-на-музыкантов-петиция-ногу-свело-noize-mc-и-других-артистов?utm_source=share_petition&utm_medium=custom_url&recruited_by_id=caf687c0-d989-11e6-bb7c-2fc8cc7c8827 [in Russian].

example is singer Iosif Kobzon, who became popular in the Soviet era. In 1994, *Kommersant* declared the singer "mobster of the year,"[94] and starting in 1995, Kobzon was barred from entering the U.S. on suspicions of ties with the Russian mob. This in no way hurt his Russian political career under Vladimir Putin, possibly even helping it: In 2007, Kobzon joined the United Russia Party and was a State Duma deputy until his death in 2018.

Many Russian cultural figures take an active part in the regime's political projects. Aside from the traditional ways of serving the ruling clan by performing at private parties and official concerts, cultural figures can also be directly involved in political activity. They sign joint letters supporting the authorities or denouncing its opponents; they take part in election campaigns; they become proxies during Vladimir Putin's elections. They broadcast ideas to the people (from pseudo-patriotism to criminal culture); they act as a cover, allegedly representing the people and the community at large in various political projects. In particular, in early 2020, some cultural figures participated in the working group that drafted the constitutional amendments. Cultural figures thus become the emotionally charged intermediaries between the authorities and the masses. For example, Yevgeny Petrosyan, Grigory Leps, and Vika Tsyganova served to mobilize the population ideologically in support of military action. Among the younger

---

94 https://www.kommersant.ru/doc/98688?ysclid=lh91ps9kfp218344103 [in Russian].

generation, the singer Shaman, with his typical Aryan looks, stood out with his song "*Ya Russkii*" (I am Russian) during the "special operation."

Among the most politically active cultural figures speaking out on behalf of the mafia clan are *Mosfilm* conglomerate general manager Karen Shakhnazarov, Hermitage director Mikhail Piotrovsky, film directors Nikita Mikhalkov and Fedor Bondarchuk, *Et Cetera* Theater artistic director Aleksandr Kalyagin, Great Moscow State Circus on Vernadsky Avenue's director Edgard Zapashny, Mikhail Boyarsky, Nikolai Rastorguyev, and many others. Most of them hold administrative jobs, which explains a great deal, because being close to power gives access to funds and administrative resources. Fedor Bondarchuk has billions at his disposal – first, as one of the founders of *Glavkino* (currently undergoing bankruptcy proceedings), then as chairman of the *Lenfilm* board of directors. In 2009, Bondarchuk took on a two-part movie project based on the Strugatsky brothers' science fiction novel *Obitaemyi ostrov* (Inhabited island). The film was not profitable, and Bondarchuk ended up in debt. After that, however, Bondarchuk used *Fond Kino* (Film Fund) subsidies. To produce the movie *Stalingrad*, Bondarchuk received around 30% ($10,000,000) of the total project cost, and 60% (around $3,500,000) for the movie *Attraction*. He says it's essentially impossible today to do without government support: so-called "soft money" (meaning government money, essentially money that doesn't have to be repaid) ensures both loans and investors.[95] Starting in 2020, Bondarchuk became the official representative of the Gazprombank brand: it's hard to imagine a more perfect symbol of culture and state-supervised business coming together. In 2014, Bondarchuk established relationships with Kovalchuk's NMG (National Media Group), too, after the media holding company NMG bought from Bondarchuk a share in a subdivision of his Art Pictures Vision company group, which produces TV movies and series.[96]

It is not, however, just a matter of the personal qualities of those cultural leaders who ensure the link between culture and politics. The setup for funding various cultural areas is such that state support is often essential; funding of the arts may disappear if the artistic product does not fall in line with the mafia state's concept. The lack of transparency of government funding mechanisms places any cultural figure at risk of facing an administrative or criminal prosecution. In taking the money, the person becomes the mafia state's hostage.

All attempts to make the Russian movie industry self-sustaining failed, and the movie industry fully depends on government funding.[97] Since 2010, the

---

95 https://www.kommersant.ru/doc/3212669 [in Russian].

96 https://www.kommersant.ru/doc/3212669 [in Russian].

97 https://vestnik.journ.msu.ru/books/2015/6/model-gosudarstvennoy-podderzhki-otechestvennoy-kinematografii-etapy-razvitiya-i-sovremennoe-sostoya/ [in Russian].

Ministry of Culture and *Fond Kino* financially support the Russian film industry. The state funds spent on producing a movie are supposed to be repaid in total or in part, but are sometimes not repaid at all. As a rule, state funding cannot exceed 70% of a film's projected cost, but may reach 100% if a film is considered to have special social significance. As a result, rules of the game in this industry completely lack transparency.[98]

In late 2012, an Auditing Chamber panel examined the results of an inquiry into how efficiently state funds were allocated to the movie industry in 2010 – 2012. The Auditing Chamber estimated that, on average, moviemakers repaid to the Film Fund a considerably lower sum than the amount that they received for producing, distributing, and showing the films. For example, in 2011, state-supported for-profit films received 4.1 billion rubles, or 72.6% of Russia cinema ticket sales, but less than 100 million rubles was returned to the Film Fund.[19] Consequently, the Auditing Chamber noted that the Film Fund "essentially subsidizes the movie industry."

Theaters are equally – or more – dependent on the state than the movie industry. For example, in 2018, over two-thirds of theaters' total income, which was over 99.5 billion rubles, was from state subsidies and

---

98 https://vestnik.journ.msu.ru/books/2015/6/model-gosudarstvennoy-podderzhki-otechestvennoy-kinematografii-etapy-razvitiya-i-sovremennoe-sostoya/ [in Russian].

grants.[99] Essentially, all theaters exist at government expense: state funds are allocated as grants and subsidies on a competitive basis. The bidding procedure is mandatory under the law on government procurement (Federal Law 44), according to which the state has to allocate the funds to the bidders who offer the best conditions (for example, the lowest job cost or the broadest spectrum of services). Theaters that win the bid must report back to the state on all funds received. The reports are sent to the Ministry of Culture, which has to examine the documents and approve them.[100]

Government subsidies do not simply create financial dependency; they are also a leash that ensures total control. A deviation from the ideological norm may result in punishment, as vividly demonstrated in the case against Moscow's Gogol-Center theater artistic director Kirill Serebrennikov. His avant-garde plays and principled social stand were enough to prosecute him on criminal grounds. Kirill Serebrennikov's case was as significant in the theater world as the Yukos Affair was in the business world. It was clear: the authorities are sending a signal once again, this time to artists. Their signal is simple, straightforward, and unequivocal: you are either on the same path as the system or you are not, and if not, then your path is known and pre-determined. In the summer of the so-called "special opera-

---

99 https://www.forbes.ru/obshchestvo/381281-teatralnyy-karman-zachem-gosudarstvo-tratit-na-teatry-69-mlrd-rubley-v-god [in Russian].

100 https://www.bbc.com/russian/45249031 [in Russian].

tion," 2022, Gogol-Center was closed, while some theaters experienced a change of management.

In May 2023, the theater world was shaken by a further blatant crackdown. Director Zhenya Berkovich and playwright Svetlana Petriichuk were arrested on suspicion of condoning terrorism in the play *Finist Yasnyi Sokol* (Finist the Brave Falcon). The play was based on Russian court documents from trials of two women who traveled to ISIS fighters in Syria after meeting them over the internet. This arrest occurred despite the fact that the same play had previously received the prestigious Russian "Golden Mask" award.

THE ROLE OF RELIGION AND THE CHURCH IN THE MAFIA STATE

As an institution, the Russian Eastern Orthodox Church [ROC] has been absorbed into secular life in modern Russia, merged with the state (despite the Constitution), often instills aggressive ideas in public consciousness, and is motivated by money. The Church plays a significant role in militarizing public consciousness. A symbol of this symbiosis between the state and the church is the Patriarchal Cathedral in the Name of the Resurrection of Christ, also known as the Main Cathedral of the Russian Armed Forces, which was built in Patriot Park. The building, pompous both inside and outside, is laced with imperial militaristic spirit, a cult of war. Only at the last minute the decision was made not to add two mosaics inside the Cathedral – one of a victory parade with Stalin's portrait, the other with images of Putin, Shoigu, Matvienko, Volodin, and Bortnikov. Both mosaics were instead placed in a museum located in Patriot Park where the cathedral stands.

The religiosity of people in Vladimir Putin's circle fully illustrates "hybrid religiousness." *Ozero* (Lake) cooperative co-founder and former Russian Railroads head Vladimir Yakunin personally delivers the Holy Flame from Jerusalem for Easter. He did that even while still head of Russian Railroads, and many believers were puzzled as to why an official is conducting such a mission. Most believe that Yakunin, who has a luxurious *dacha* with fur storage, resigned due to suspicions of corruption, siphoning company funds to offshores, and because his son applied for British citizenship.[101] This does not stop Yakunin from continuing his religious activity and transporting the Holy Flame.

Another example is Konstantin Goloshchapov, the Rotenberg brothers' business partner and a Russian Athos Society founder. Goloshchapov met Putin and Arkady Rotenberg in the 1980s, when they trained in judo together. Goloshchapov even brought his buddy Vladimir Kumarin to work out at Rotenberg's gym. Later, Kumarin changed his last name to Barsukov and became a Tambov mob boss, the head of gangster St. Petersburg. In 1998, a year and a half after Putin moved to Moscow, Goloshchapov became general manager of the President's Administrative Department's *Rostsentrproekt* Federal State Unitary Enterprise. Since then, Goloshchapov has held various positions, but the basis of his prosperity is his partnership with the Rotenbergs.

According to *Agentstvo politicheskikh novostei* (Political News Agency), by the early 2000s, Goloshchapov organized special trips to Athos for some of Putin's "St. Petersburg crew." During those trips, they had time to pray and to make various important decisions. After Putin's visit to Athos in 2005, Goloshchapov and a group of his friends founded the Russian Athos Society. The society's board of trustees was star-studded: Poltavchenko, Luzhkov, Chemezov, Lavrov. Many prominent individuals had ties to the Athos Society: the

---

101 https://pasmi.ru/archive/129483/ [in Russian].

Rotenberg brothers, former General Prosecutor Yuri Chaika, Vladimir Yakunin, Minister of Emergency Situations Sergei Shoigu [currently defense minister]. The Society's official purpose is developing ties with monks at the sacred Mount Athos, organizing pilgrimages there, restoring monasteries and churches on Athos and in Russia. In fact, however, it is a private elite club for government officials and businessmen, and very secular business matters were handled during trips to Athos. Goloshchapov became an intermediary who was a member of Putin's circle and also close to top brass at the Russian Orthodox Church. All this was, of course, before the February full-scale invasion.

The trips to Athos, however, were just an individual way of joining the narrow circle of Putin's elite. The church became a genuine and important element of the mafia state under Patriarch Kirill, who occupied the post in 2009 after the death of Aleksey II. Kirill is one of Metropolitan Nikodim (Rotov)'s favorite students. In his book *Russkaia pravoslavnaia tserkov: sovremennoe sostoyanie i problemy)* (The Russian Orthodox Church: Current Condition and Problems), sociologist and Russian Orthodox Church researcher Nikolai Mitrokhin identifies a group he calls "right-wing Nikodim supporters," who share Metropolitan Nikodim's desire to take an active part in public life, his "statist" views, and the view that the state must closely collaborate with the church. Kirill was the most visible figure in this group. "Right-wing Nikodim supporters" perceive statist ideology as an acknowledgement of Russia's special path and the Russian people's fundamental role.

Under Patriarch Kirill, the church and the state became ever closer. *Conservative views based on patriarchal values, including respect for authority of the "father" both at the familial and state level, appeals to a communal collectivist mindset, and countering the West's "heresy" all perfectly suit a mafia state's goals.* Patriarch Kirill constantly calls on the faithful to vote in elections, thus raising the percentage of the anti-western, conservatively-minded electorate. He also approved of amendments to the Constitution and supported the invasion of Ukraine. The church patriarchate closely cooperates with the presidential administration and other mafia state members. In turn, the state supports construction of new churches and ensures property transfers to the Church. According to Patriarch Kirill, Russia builds three cathedrals a day.

By RBC [RosBusiness consulting located in Moscow] estimates, in 2012-2015 alone, the Russian Orthodox Church and related groups received at least 14 billion rubles. From the state budget and governmental organizations. In particular, in 2014-2015, over 1.8 billion rubles was allocated to Russian Orthodox Church organizations to set up and develop Russian spiritual and educational centers under the federal program called "Strengthening the unity of the Russian nation and ethno-cultural development of Russia's peoples."[102]

---

102 https://www.rbc.ru/investigation/society/24/02/2016/56c84fd49a7947ecbff1473d?ysclid=lkv38qha2u325855121 [in Russian].

Permanent members of the Holy Synod enjoy privileges granted primarily by the RF presidential administrative office. For example, in February 2016, Patriarch Kirill flew to Latin America, and visited Paraguay, Chile, Brazil and even Antarctica. Notably, he traveled by *Rossiya* special flight squad jetliner. The flight squad reports to the RF Presidential Administration Department and serves the state's top brass. The Patriarch's security is handled by the Federal Security Guard Service.

Spiritual leaders play a special role in Russia's regime. Metropolitan Tikhon (Shevkunov) is called "Putin's Spiritual Guide" and is said to have a certain influence on Putin. Metropolitan Tikhon does not confirm this, but he does admit meeting with the president. From 1995 to 2018, Archimandrite Tikhon, formerly a graduate of the All-Russian State Institute of Cinematography's filmmaking department, was the Superior at Moscow's Sretensky Monastery located in the city center on Bolshaya Lubyanka St. Another parishioner of Tikhon's was Vladimir Ustinov, even when he served as prosecutor general. After a burglary at the monastery, Archimandrite Tikhon called Ustinov directly. The media noted that Rosneft head Igor Sechin is also acquainted with Tikhon. Tikhon also has a good relationship with former FSB head, Security Council secretary Nikolai Patrushev.[103]

---

103 http://politcom.ru/22863.html [in Russian].

Tikhon told an FT journalist that he met Putin in 1999,[104] and in 2000, Tikhon already accompanied Putin on a visit to Pskovo-Pechersky Monastery.[105]

Since 2018, Tikhon is Metropolitan of Pskov and Porkhovo. His views are very conservative, anti-Western, and anti-liberal; he calls for a revival of ideology in the state and actively works to that end by overseeing projects at the intersection of history and propaganda, such as the "Russia – My History" theme parks. During Putin's sudden visit to Crimea in March 2023, Putin visited the historic and archeological Tauric Chersonesos Park in Sevastopol, where Metropolitan Tikhon met him. The park is one of Tikhon's projects, and it was funded by "friends" at *Transneft* and *Gazprom neft*.[106]

---

104 https://www.ft.com/content/f2fcba3e-65be-11e2-a3db-00144feab49a.

105 https://istories.media/investigations/2022/08/01/propagandist-ot-boga/?ysclid=lhahzakl9k748383746.

106 https://www.kommersant.ru/doc/5886563?ysclid=lhahwvaz3j494265959.

The mafia state against civil society in Russia

The mafia state has a rather primitive attitude toward civil society: it must be controlled, and it must act in accordance with the regime's interests. It is not the job of civil society to represent citizens' interests, or, even worse, implement public oversight of the government and participate in governance. There are zones, "reservations," where non-profit organizations and volunteers are welcomed and rewarded, or where barriers and complications do not put an end to their work, such as social or charitable affairs or the spheres of, medicine, and science. Civil society thus is left with performing the functions and filling the niches that do not receive sufficient attention from the state.

Such non-profit organizations have been supported by the Russian state since 2006. Initially, the Public Chamber and the presidential administration distributed the grants, but starting in 2007, this authority was given to special grant-distributing organizations, which themselves are non-profits working in various areas. An analysis done by the *Autonomous Non-Profit Organization, Transparency International – R Center for Anti-Corruption Research and Initiatives* examined grant distribution for the year 2012 and concluded that the setup completely lacks transparency, with money going to organizations linked to the Public Chamber or other state entities as a result. The fund's distribution structure changed in 2017. The Presidential Grant Fund became the sole operator of the state's support for non-profits.

The state regards any manifestations of civil society outside the framework of its specific niches as potentially harmful and dangerous. Independent non-profits and activists were pressured, and many had to stop their activity. The regime uses several "official" tools to achieve their goal: declaring an organization or an individual a "foreign agent," bringing charges of extremism, and labeling Western human rights organizations as "undesirable" in Russia.

The term an "undesirable organization" appeared in 2015, when a law was passed forbidding activity of "undesirable" foreign or international organizations in Russia. Any foreign organization can be labeled "undesirable," after which all its activities in Russia are forbidden. Russian citizens face first administrative, then criminal liability for collaborating with such an organization.

The Law on Foreign Agents was adopted earlier, in 2012. This law obligated NGOs that engaged in political activity and received funding from abroad to register as "foreign agents." The Ministry of Justice keeps a special foreign agent list. In 2020, a law was passed under which individuals, too, could be labeled "foreign agents." This was an attack on human rights activists and journalists. One of the first people to land on the list was former *Za Prava Cheloveka* (For Human Rights) movement leader Lev Ponomarev.

Foreign agents must present reports on their activities and documents on received funds and expenditures, and any informational materials they disseminate must contain the notation "published by an organization that serves the functions of a foreign agent." For many non-profits subsisting on grants and already experiencing difficulties with funding, this law became a "guilty" verdict. Organizations reacted in various ways: some refused Western grants, others shut down and formed new organizations, still others did whatever they could in order to be removed from the "foreign agent" list.

The mafia state, however, did not stop there. Before the September 2021 elections, a law was passed hurriedly that further protected the political arena from opponents. People nicknamed it "the law against the Anti-Corruption Foundation and against Navalny's supporters." The law bars members of "extremist and terrorist" organizations from running for office; at the same time, it classified as such anyone who showed support with words (including on the web), funding or other assistance to such an entity. At the time this law was adopted, the prosecutor's office demanded that the Anti-Corruption Foundation and a network of Navalny's offices be recognized as "extremist." This law meant that the people who ran the foundation's offices were banned from taking part in elections. Any of Navalny's supporters may lose their right to run for office if a court so rules: it's enough to repost or "like" a post on social media, or to send funds in support.

Naturally, the mafia state arsenal includes direct crackdowns on political activists. According to March

2019 data, there were 236 political prisoners in Russia, including those on the Crimean Peninsula. This is according to the "The Kremlin's Political Prisoners: Advancing a Political Agenda by Crushing Dissent,"[107] compiled by the U.S. law firm Perseus Strategies with the participation of the Russian Memorial Human Rights Centre. The number of political prisoners in Russia increased significantly in comparison with prior years: in 2015, Memorial counted 46 political prisoners in Russia. Most of those serving sentences were jailed for exercising rights guaranteed by international law. Others were convicted on charges of crimes that "they simply did not commit" (murder, sexual assault, espionage, and some other types of crime). Memorial itself was pressured, too. In early 2022, Memorial, whose roster of founders included Andrei Sakharov, was shut down by court decision.

107 https://www.perseus-strategies.com/wp-content/uploads/2019/04/The-Kremlins-Political-Prisoners-May-2019.pdf

Control over public opinion

May 2019 was not easy for the regime. An All-Russian Public Opinion Research Center (Russian acronym: VTsIOM) poll showed that Vladimir Putin's confidence rating dropped to 31.7%, the lowest in 13 years. Although it was Putin's rating that dropped, it was VTsIOM leadership that was held responsible. Putin's press secretary Dmitry Peskov announced that the Kremlin expects sociologists to analyze the correlation of the data. "How can confidence ratings be down when electoral ratings are up?" – Peskov asked. That can be explained, however: when there is no choice, you have to vote for whatever is there, even if you have no confidence in that person. The outcome of the analysis was a change in VTsIOM methodology. Instead of asking "In which politicians do you have confidence?" the question now was: "Do you have confidence in Vladimir Putin?" This new methodology raised the confidence rating to 72.3%.

As a science, sociology studies society and social processes, and explains social phenomena. As an applied science, sociology makes it possible to predict and manage social phenomena. In a mafia state, both functions are subject to distortions. In Russia, there's even "secret sociology" that has existed since the Soviet period. Analytical material on trends in society, citizens' attitudes, and the population's views on certain issues are prepared for the presidential administration by the Federal Protection Service staff. It is rather difficult to gain access to these materials; the information is confidential, although sometimes there are media leaks.

Several large public-access sociology institutes operate in Russia: the state-controlled VTsIOM; the state-controlled Public Opinion Foundation; the independent Levada Center created by former VTsIOM staff who left after a change in leadership, when political scientist Valery Fedorov was appointed director; and the private research holding company Romir, which started in sociological monitoring but moved more toward doing marketing research. In 1999, VTsIOM, Romir and the Public Opinion Foundation all contributed to Putin's election as president. In 1999, moreover, it was shown that poll data interpretation was equally important, if not more important, than the poll data itself.

In spring 1999, VTsIOM and Romir asked the Russian people: "For which movie hero would you vote for President?"[108] The top four were Gleb Zheglov from the crime romance novel,[109] the romantic World War II spy Stierlitz (Maksim Maksimovich Isaev) [110], the legend-

---

108 https://www.kommersant.ru/doc/15481 [in Russian].

109 Gleb Zheglov is a fictional crime-solving detective featured in the popular 1979 mystery TV series *Mesto vstrechi izmenit nelzya* ("The Meeting Place Cannot be Changed") played by the popular actor Vladimir Vysotsky.

110 Max Otto von Stierlitz (Maksim Maksimovich Isayev) is a fictional character in numerous works by the Soviet author Yulian Semyonov and lead character of the TV series *Semnadtzat mgnovenii vesny* ("Seventeen Moments of Spring"). Stierlitz became the most famous image of a spy in Soviet and post-Soviet culture.

ary World War II hero Marshal Zhukov, and the mythic, heroic Russian leader Peter the Great. Romir analysts concluded: "When it comes to leading the nation, most Russians are prepared to have an aggressive leader instead of a caring one. People prefer strength and cruelty, expecting that these qualities will help establish order in Russia." Although VTsIOM's poll showed Stierlitz in fourth place, and Romir's poll showed him in second place, it was announced to the nation that " Stierlitz is our president," and it was Stierlitz's image that appeared on the cover of *Kommersant-Vlast* magazine with the caption that read "President-2000." When the poll was conducted, Putin was simultaneously head of the FSB and Security Council secretary. He was the one who fit Stierlitz's image.

Those first elections showed Putin the importance of sociology. Naturally, this sector was placed under state control. First, they replaced the head of VTsIOM. In 2003, Yuri Levada, who had headed the center since 1992, was removed and replaced with a young political scientist, Valery Fedorov, who previously had worked at the Centre for Political Trends that conducted projects commissioned by the presidential administration. Since then, VTsIOM performs specific tasks: ensuring propagandist campaigns and checking the population's reactions to the regime's decisions or ideas.

Yuri Levada and his team founded the alternative, independent Levada Center. Lev Gudkov, who became head of Levada Center in 2006 after Levada's death, explained an approach to sociology as follows: "Orwell described such a thing as *doublethink*. Voting "for" can very well coincide with a high degree of disdain and disrespect for the regime. Therefore, what we provide is, first of all, various interpretations of sociological processes. Sociology is not questionnaires and polls – sociology is precisely interpretation, analysis, a certain view of societal processes."[111]

In 2013, Levada Center showed that protest attitudes were strong in society, that Putin's ratings were dropping, and discontent was growing over the state of affairs in the country. After publishing these findings, the Center became the subject of frequent inspections, including visits from the Ministry of Justice, the Prosecutor's Office, the Tax Service, the Interior Ministry, and the Department for Fighting Extremism. A new wave started in 2016 when the language of the law governing non-profits was changed: previously, sociological polls were not considered to be political activity, but under the amended law they were now categorized as political activity. Levada Center was labeled a "foreign agent," and its finances took a hit, as the number of commercial orders dropped. Moreover, the Center could no longer publish data during elections campaigns, because, as a foreign agent, they were prohibited from "interfering with the political process."

---

111 https://elementy.ru/nauchno-populyarnaya_biblioteka/434098/Nezavisimoy_sotsiologii_v_Rossii_net [in Russian].

The mafia state's economy

Property redistribution started as soon as Putin came to power in Russia. In a mafia state, nationalization is a legal method for the mafia to gain control over assets. Under the banner of "state interests," the mafia group ensures themselves a source of income. Hostile takeovers become state-sponsored and reach an entirely new level.

Even official data are impressive. The state sector started growing in the 2000s, and reached "exceptionally high levels," says a Federal Antimonopoly Service (FAS) report on the state of competition for 2018.[112] Prior to the 1998 financial crisis, the state's share of the Russian economy was estimated at around 25%. In 2008, it reached 40-45%, by 2013, it exceeded 50%. In 2017, many experts said it reached 60-70%, with no significant change in 2018 and 2019.[113]

The state prioritizes amassing and controlling property without regard for efficiency. A Center for Strategic Research report cited by FAS notes: "In areas of financial efficiency, state-owned companies lag behind private companies." FAS concluded: "The process of strengthening the state's role in the Russian economy has taken a different qualitative form. This occurs through increasing the state entities' role in distributing finan-

---

112 https://fas.gov.ru/documents/685806 [in Russian].

113 https://fas.gov.ru/documents/685806 [in Russian] .

cial resources, controlling economic agents, activating state companies and development institutions, transferring non-public state-owned companies to them, 'pseudo privatization' processes, and expanding government regulation areas." Merging monopolies with the state, outright nationalization of production, and an increase in distributed government contracts are integral features of the Russian economy.

Mafia state methods: forcible re-privatization

When you have an entire state at your disposal, the arsenal of methods for property redistribution is almost limitless, although those methods most of all resemble a hostile takeover.

The process started in Russia in 2003, when the Yukos Affair became a historic turning point. At the time, Yukos was one the country's largest companies, a leader in instilling Western standards of transparency, and a leader in efficiency. *Ekspert* magazine rated Yukos fourth in sales among Russia's largest companies (after Gazprom, RAO Unified System of Russia and Lukoil), although Yukos rated above Lukoil for pretax income.[114] Yukos was the fastest-growing Russian oil company. In 2003, Yukos was the leading oil producer. It was announced that Yukos would merge with Sibneft, which the Kremlin seemed to have approved. Typical of a mafia state, a "special operation" was used to take over Yukos in pursuit of several interests and aspirations: taking control over the

114 https://expert.ru/ratings/e400-2003/ [in Russian].

country's largest oil company and punishing Yukos head Mikhail Khodorkovsky for his political ambitions and for his publicly pointing out to Putin personally that there is corruption in the industry. Yukos was saddled with tax bills in the billions; it declared bankruptcy, and its assets were sold, mostly to Rosneft, at minimal prices. Mikhail Khodorkovsky and his Yukos partner Platon Lebedev were arrested and spent 10 years in prison.

The Yukos Affair became a model for hostile takeovers by the state – a comprehensive approach to seizing assets using law enforcement and administrative resources. The show trials of Mikhail Khodorkovsky, Platon Lebedev and other Yukos Affair victims made it easier for the state to deal with large business in the future and to force them to surrender assets. Whereas the symbol of the relationship between the state and the business circles of the 1990s were loans-for-shares auctions, the first 20 years of the twenty-first century in Russia were marked by *forcible re-privatization.*

For example, privately-owned Bashneft became the property of state-owned Rosneft, which took Bashneft's most attractive assets: the oil refineries in Bashkiria and the license to develop the large Trebs and Titov oil fields (in partnership with Lukoil). In the early 2010s, Bashneft was owned by Vladimir Yevtushenkov's *Sistema* JSFC (Joint-Stock Financial Corporation). In 2014, however, investigators decided that former Bashkiria President Murtaza Rakhimov's son Ural Rakhimov and his partner conspired in the 2000s to embezzle the majority share of Bashneft and Ufa-based oil refineries. The stocks were sold for $2.5 billion to *Sistema* JSFC and other companies. A criminal case was initiated against Rakhimov for embezzlement (misappropriation) and money laundering. In September 2014, while working on this case, the Investigative Committee charged *Sistema* owner Yevtushenkov with money laundering, placed him under house arrest, and froze *Sistema*-held Bashneft stock (71%). The General Prosecutor's Office reclaimed the share package, and it became state property. Despite the absurdity of the situation, the commercial court ruled in favor of the General Prosecutor's Office, and Bashneft stock was simply seized from *Sistema*, with 50.08% going to the state represented by *Rosimushchestvo* (Russian Federal Agency for State Property Management) and 25% to Bashkortostan. Two years later, Rosneft bought 50.08% of Bashneft shares for 329.7 billion rubles. This was called "privatization." In 2017, Rosneft, in another unprecedented move, accused *Sistema* of depreciating the value of the shares and sued Yevtushenkov's company for 136.4 billion rubles. The case was eventually settled out of court, with *Sistema* agreeing to pay 100 billion rubles.[115] Yevtushenkov lost the asset and the money, but avoided jail, and kept his other businesses, including the cell phone provider MTS.

Even tougher methods were used to appropriate assets in occupied territories. *Vazhnye istorii* (Important stories)[116] learned that Putin's friends became the main

---

115 https://tass.ru/ekonomika/4837300?ysclid=lkv3kl-9v3o88728424 [in Russian].

116 An independent media website specializing in investigative journalism; it is now located in Latvia.

owners of Ukraine's nationalized property in Crimea. After the peninsula was annexed, part of what was taken was put up for privatization. Yuri Kovalchuk was the main purchaser, acquiring real estate, land, and wineries.

Mafia state methods: forced deals

In a mafia state, property may be owned only as long as the state permits. After that, conditions may be created that will force the property owner to sell. This is more or less what happened with Yandex, as described above.

Another example is Itera, one of the few independent gas producers in Russia at the time. It did quite well in the 1990s and early 2000s as an intermediary for Turkmen gas shipments to the Ukrainian market.

Itera ran into roadblocks, however, when it tried getting into gas production in Russia. For years, Itera couldn't get Gazprom to agree to connect the Beregovoye field to the gas pipeline. As Gazprom owns the gas pipeline system in Russia, independent producers need Gazprom management's agreement to use the pipeline to send gas to their customers. Gazprom was not signing agreements with Itera, the ready-to-use field stood idle, and license holders suffered losses. Gas shipments started only after Gazprombank obtained the majority share of Sibneftegaz (Sibneftegaz, which was co-owned by Itera and a partner, held the license for the oilfield). Although the transaction amount was not disclosed, there was talk in the market that the Sibneftegaz majority stake was sold at a great discount.[117] Thus, Itera first lost its main asset, then ceased to exist in 2013 when Rosneft bought it.

In November 2007, *Kommersant* newspaper published probably the most scandalous interview in the history of Russian business journalism. *Finansgrupp* (Finance Group) FIG (Financial-Industrial Group) head Oleg Shvartzman suddenly decided to be frank, relating that presidential administration *siloviki* bloc members' relatives are behind his companies.[118] Shvartzman openly described the method that became the foundation of Putin's mafia state, explaining the "party politics:" "We don't take enterprises; we minimize their market value using various tools, usually voluntary-forcible tools. There is a market value, and there are techniques to block its growth, using various administrative means of course. As a rule, however, people understand where we are coming from...." The "gang" was personified by head of the *siloviki* bloc Igor Sechin. The business circles' reaction showed that Shvartzman's story was remarkably close to the truth.

Mafia state methods: the mafia must get its cut

Leonid Mikhelson and Gennady Timchenko's partnership in Novatek (which turned out to be highly profitable) could be considered as originally forced to some

---

117 https://www.kommersant.ru/doc/686590 [in Russian]

118 https://www.kommersant.ru/doc/831089 [in Russian]

extent. Mikhelson, who began his business in Samara, started looking for partners as soon as his company became a notable independent gas producer. First, he unsuccessfully tried to merge with Itera, but the merger was called off. Then, in 2004, Agreement was reached on selling a blocking stake to the French company *Total* for $800 million, but FAS delayed signing off on the deal, and it fell through. This turned out to be to Mikhelson's benefit. He changed his partner-seeking strategy, first selling a stake in Novatek to Gazprom, then partnering with Gennady Timchenko. Only after all these deals did *Total* finally become a Novatek shareholder in 2011. Mikhelson became one of the officially richest people in Russia. This case showed that success in Russia is possible thanks to partnership with and loyalty to the mafia circle.

Mafia state methods: "effective" buyout

Mergers and acquisitions are also governed by mafia logic. Some businessmen's assets are simply seized or bought for pennies on the dollar, whereas others' assets are bought for record high sums, prompting the suspicion of hidden motives and mechanisms for such deals. The first example is Roman Abramovich, who in 2005 sold Sibneft to Gazprom for an unheard-of price at the time – $13 billion. Rosneft also spared no expense when buying TNK-BP in 2012. For its share, British BP received $16.65 billion in cash as well as a 12.84% share of Rosneft, while the AAR consortium received $27.73 billion.

By the end of Putin's 20 years in power, his closest associates started leaving the construction business for a number of reasons. Large-scale construction ended, e.g., stadiums for the world championship and the first stage of *Sila Sibiri* (Siberian Strength) gas pipeline. New projects became problematic due to U.S. and European sanctions. When a company has its own staff and its own technology, there are constant expenses for upkeep and amortization. In 2019, Arkady Rotenberg sold *Stroigazmontazh* to an unknown company called *Stroyinvestholding* for 75 billion rubles.

It was later learned that *Stroigazmontazh* was bought by Gazprom subsidiary *Gazstroiprom* and a Gazprombank outfit.[119] For the sake of comparison, Arkady Rotenberg's entities had bought from Gazprom the five companies that formed the basis for *Stroigazmontazh* for 8.3 billion rubles in 2008.

In 2020, Gazprom-affiliated companies also bought *Stroitransneftegaz* from Gennady Timchenko and his partners. The value of the deal was not disclosed, but media sources said it was 30billion rubles. Admittedly, a construction company is worth only as much as the contracts it brings in. In the 2000s, construction divisions were deemed non-core assets for Gazprom, and Gazprom sold them, with some going to Putin's friends. Later, when the time came to buy the assets back from Putin's friends, these assets were no longer considered non-core. The well-known rule of a mafia state's exis-

---

119 https://www.rbc.ru/business/07/11/2019/5dc435e29a7947503d73b369?ysclid=lkwj0vfocb274911182 [in Russian].

tence is: "privatizing profits, nationalizing losses," or, in simpler words: "The state pays expenses, and we pocket the income."

Mafia state methods: taking control over key assets

As soon as he took office, Vladimir Putin started putting his own people in control of key state assets, and control over financial flows went to the "right" people. Replacing Viktor Chernomyrdin, the founding father of Gazprom and essentially of the entire Russian gas industry, 34-year-old Dmitry Medvedev became chairman of the Gazprom board of directors. At the time, Medvedev was deputy head of the presidential administration. Earlier, he had been Putin's colleague at Smolny and was Putin's future alternate in the "tandem" format. Less than a year later, Gazprom chairman of the management board Rem Vyakhirev lost his position and was replaced by Aleksey Miller, the 39-year-old deputy minister of energy, who had also worked with Putin at St. Petersburg City Hall and for a while was Putin's deputy at the foreign affairs committee.

The personnel changes looked like a special operation: 64-year-old Vyakhirev learned that he was being removed early in the morning of May 30, 2001, from Putin himself, in Putin's Kremlin office. Putin thanked Vyakhirev for his work, and told Vyakhirev that his contract that was set to expire the next day, May 31, would not be renewed.[120] Putin then summoned all Gazprom board of directors' members to the Kremlin and announced that Vyakhirev was leaving and Miller was arriving. Miller's appointment seemed strange, as Miller had no connection to the gas industry and appeared too inexperienced and too much of a lightweight to manage the "generals" – directors of Gazprom local subsidiaries. Miller had one quality – he was a 100% insider.

A joke was popular at the time that reflected the randomness of Miller's becoming the new big boss:

"There's a meeting in Putin's office about who should become head of Gazprom. It's hot in the office. Putin wants to refresh himself with a beer and asks his assistants to "go get me 'Miller'!" The assistants misunderstood, and thus Aleksey Miller became head of Gazprom."

The media noted that Miller coordinated even the smallest details with Putin directly, to say nothing of staff appointments.[121] Miller carried out at least one task: he "purged" the staff, with all key posts, primarily anything involving finance, going to Miller's people. Elena Vasilieva, who used to work for Miller at the St. Petersburg Seaport, became Gazprom's chief accountant. Another former subordinate of Miller's at the Port, and one of the people closest to him, is Kirill Seleznev.

---

120 https://www.vedomosti.ru/newspaper/articles/2009/04/20/hroniki-20012009-gg-davi-na-gaz [in Russian].

121 https://www.vedomosti.ru/newspaper/articles/2009/04/20/hroniki-20012009-gg-davi-na-gaz [in Russian]

Seleznev was first appointed Miller's assistant, but soon joined the Gazprom management board and became general manager of *Mezhregiongaz*. The management board staff was headed by Mikhail Sereda, Miller's colleague at Baltic Pipe System (where Miller was general manager from 1999-2000); 32-year-old Andrei Kruglov, who had worked at St. Petersburg City Hall for a few years, was appointed head of Corporate Finance and was soon promoted to Gazprom CFO.

Almost immediately after Miller arrived, Aleksandr Dybal became head of the Gazprom informational policy department. Dybal was a media manager from St. Petersburg, who in 1996 had helped provide informational support for then-mayor Anatoly Sobchak's election campaign. In 2001, Dmitry Medvedev's classmate Konstantin Chuichenko became head of the Gazprom legal department and joined the management board. In January 2020, Chuichenko became RF Justice Minister. In 2003, one of *Ozero* cooperative founders Sergei Fursenko was appointed deputy head of the Gazprom Department of Gas Transport, Underground Storage and Use, and from July 2003 to 2008, Fursenko was general manager of Gazprom subsidiary *Lentransgaz*.

In 2007, Boris Nemtsov and Vladimir Milov wrote in their report "Putin and Gazprom": "Today, 11 out of 18 company management board members holding the most important positions – in supervising finances, property, and corporate governance – are people who in the 1990s worked either in the St. Petersburg administration, St. Petersburg Seaport OJSC, other St. Petersburg businesses, or the FSB." One of the last to join Miller's team was Vladimir Putin's first cousin once removed Mikhail Putin. Starting in 2007, Mikhail Putin was both deputy chairman of SOGAZ and Miller's advisor, and in 2018 Mikhail Putin was appointed deputy chairman of the Gazprom management board. And these are just the most notable appointments.

During the 20 years that Putin's inner circle controlled Gazprom, executive salaries grew exponentially. The number of members on the management board and the board of directors did not change radically, and board of directors members do not receive remuneration from the state for their work.

From 2001 to 2019, members of the Gazprom management board and board of directors received a total of 29.5 billion rubles. That is divided among fewer than 30 people. This amount reflects only remuneration for working at the parent company; as there is additional income from being on subsidiaries' boards of directors, the overall total is a bit higher.

Mafia state methods: taking control of the banking sector

The banking sector was nationalized under the pretext of improved reliability and invigoration. The special 2018 RF Government Analytical Center report titled "Can Private Banks Survive?" cites the following data: among the largest banks, practically no private lending institutions remained; state-owned banks' share in lending to companies exceeded 80%, and in lending to individuals, it is over 70%.[122]

Consolidating and nationalizing the bank system through a "big cleanup" was activated in November 2013. Over the following four and a half years, (as of August 1, 2018), 358 bank licenses were rescinded, which is more than had been rescinded in the prior 9 years.[123] One in four large Russian banks ceased to exist.

The situation worsened when, in 2017, the Central Bank started using a new bailout mechanism through the Bank Sector Consolidation Fund. Using this Fund, the Central Bank itself became owner of the banks being bailed out, thus creating an oligopoly in the financial market that benefits state-owned banks, as the Central Bank not only regulates but also owns large lending institutions.[124]

A conflict of interest is typical of any sector with a high percentage of state ownership because the state is both a player and a regulator. No matter how you look at it, state-owned companies have a significant advantage over private players. This was especially evident in the bank sector: *the state provided large-scale assistance to state-owned banks while destroying nonstate owned banks.* State-

---

122 https://ac.gov.ru/archive/files/publication/a/17898.pdf [in Russian].

123 https://ac.gov.ru/archive/files/publication/a/17898.pdf [in Russian].

124 https://publications.hse.ru/articles/399350792 [in Russian].

owned banks have much easier access to administrative resources than do private banks. For example, during the 2008 economic crisis, the state allocated almost a trillion rubles in subordinated loans for banks' top-up capitalization: Sberbank received 500 billion rubles from the Central Bank, *Vneshtorgbank* (Bank for Foreign Trade) and *Rosselkhozbank* received 225 billion rubles from *Vneshekonombank* (Bank for Foreign Economic Activity). *Vneshekonombank* held the same amount ready for large private banks, but only on the condition that shareholders match the new capital (in the end, *Vneshekonombank* provided around 90 billion rubles).[125]

In Russia's bank market, access to state resources thus becomes the main criterion instead of quality of service.

Nationalizing the banking sector has grave consequences for the economy and involves a number of serious risks. Such a bank system model loses the ability flexibly to adapt to the market's changing needs. In the end, the bank sector no longer meets the needs of certain segments and market niches in the real economic sector, which, in the worst-case scenario, can provoke the development of a quasi-bank services market.[126] Monopolizing the sector means less choice for customers in choosing organizations, limited access to lending, the deterioration of service conditions, and lower-quality service.

---

125 https://www.vedomosti.ru/finance/articles/2019/10/29/814907-20-let-rossiya?ysclid=lheqa1u67t314295350 [in Russian].

126 https://ac.gov.ru/archive/files/publication/a/17898.pdf [in Russian].

In a crisis situation, the state must support state-owned banks, which may result in high expenditures.

As a result, customers often decide to bank with "system" banks, and a smaller number of large banks is easier to control.

Mafia state methods: focus on raw materials

The Yukos Affair became a prologue to essentially nationalizing the oil industry and transferring control over it to the ruling clan. Rosneft obtained most of Yukos' assets, including its main producer Yuganskneftegaz and several refineries, for pennies on the dollar. Rosneft later absorbed TNK-BP and Bashneft. Gazprom received Sibneft, which became the basis for Gazprom Neft. A series of smaller absorptions also took place. *Vedomosti* newspaper wrote: "Companies that are directly or indirectly controlled by the state extract over 50%; the definitive leader with a 40% share for the nine months of 2019 is Rosneft, although its share in the early 2000s was just 4%."[127] Lukoil is basically the only independent oil company left in Russia. There's also Surgutneftegaz, but it has a non-transparent ownership structure, and it is believed to have ties to, or act in the interests of, people from Putin's closest circle. In particular, people from Surgutneftegaz created the shell company Baikalfinansgrupp that bought Yuganskneftegaz.[128]

---

127 https://www.vedomosti.ru/business/articles/2019/10/15/813716-gosudarstvo-20-let [in Russian].

128 https://www.newsru.com/finance/28jul2014/baikalfinansgrp.html [in Russian].

Unlike the oil industry (in which, when Putin came to power, private players predominated and competition existed), the gas market was monopolized from the start by Gazprom. In the early 2000s, there was serious discussion of reforming the industry, including possibly splitting Gazprom. Segregating the transport component from the conglomerate would create equal conditions for accessing pipelines for all market participants, including the few independent gas producers. These proposals never materialized, however, and the state took over the independent producers: Rosneft bought Itera; Gazprom and Gennady Timchenko bought shares in Novatek, while Gazprom and Novatek split Nortgaz. At present, only Rosneft and Lukoil are independent gas producers.

A 2005 law stipulates that the state must hold at least 50% plus one share in Gazprom. This process was officially completed only in 2013: State-owned Rosneftegaz bought 10.96% of Gazprom shares in several stages, increasing the state's share to 50.005%. A 2006 law established Gazprom's export monopoly. By controlling Gazprom, the state has access to its financial flows and can utilize Gazprom in political games instead of in shareholders' interests. This was especially apparent after the February full-scale invasion of Ukraine, when, before the 2022 heating season, Gazprom stopped gas shipments to Europe via the North Stream pipeline, saying the last working turbine was out of order at the *Portovaya* compressor station.

Gazprom is frequently criticized for failing to represent its shareholders' interests, but criticism is impermissible.

In 2018, analyst Aleksandr Fek was fired from Sberbank CIB for proposing (and proving) in his report the thesis that Gazprom's investment program is most easily understood as a method for contractors to make money to the detriment of shareholders. "*Sila Sibiri, Severny Potok-2* and *Turetzki Potok* are unprofitable, destroying the company's value with projects that will swallow up half of Gazprom's investments over the next five years. These projects are usually seen as having been forced on Gazprom by the government in pursuit of geopolitical goals. More importantly, they share another feature: the ability to provide work to a small group of Russian suppliers with essentially no external oversight," the report stated.[129]

For example, the *Sila Sibiri* (Siberian Strength) gas pipeline was chosen instead of the less-costly Altai project: $55.4 billion. Vs. $10 billion. Analysts believe *Sila Sibiri* might have been chosen because it benefited Gazprom's main contractors – Stroitransneftegaz (formerly Stroitransgaz CJSC where Timchenko held a share, and Stroigazmontazh, each receiving around half of the main *Sila Sibiri* contracts. Aleksandr Fek wrote in his report that cost him his job: "The bigger the project, the more profitable the contracts. Alas, none of these companies is traded publicly; therefore one cannot invest in them."[130]

---

129 https://globalstocks.ru/skandalnyiy-doklad-sberbank-cib-o-gazprome/ [in Russian]

130 https://globalstocks.ru/skandalnyiy-doklad-sberbank-cib-o-gazprome/ [in Russian]

A couple of years earlier, Aleksandr Branis, the director of Prosperity Capital investment company, which is a minority shareholder of Gazprom, told Putin essentially the same thing at the *Rossiya Zovet* (Russia is Calling) Forum: "Sometimes one has the impression that for some reason the company works for neither its shareholders, nor consumers, nor the state, essentially working for its subcontractors, who build various facilities for themselves. Over these 11 years, they invested $200 billion – that's a serious amount – in expanding pipelines and exploring new oilfields. That's not even counting the $80 billion simply for the facilities' upkeep. We are seeing that now all these facilities are used at 60-65% of their capacity at most."[131]

Mafia state methods: state contracts as the main source of income distribution

The king of state contracts, oligarch Arkady Rotenberg (honored with the Hero of Labor title; owner of the "palace" in Gelendzhik[132]), is a symbol of the mafia state just as the reputed super-worker Stakhanov was a symbol

131 http://www.kremlin.ru/events/president/news/53077 [in Russian].

132 According to a video produced by opposition leader Aleksei Navalny in 2021, Putin is the real owner of an enormous, elaborate Italian -"palace" near the Black Sea, which cost $956 million to build. Putin denied the story, and Rotenberg subsequently claimed to be the owner.

in the USSR.[133] Rotenberg holds the record for acquiring the most state funds. For several years, *Forbes* magazine analyzed funds distribution in Russia via state contracting. The first *Forbes* "Kings of State Contracts" list was published in 2012 and included data on state contracts concluded over the four years of Dmitry Medvedev's presidency. The last list was published in 2018, including annual data through the end of 2017. Subsequently, it became impossible to make such calculations, as a newly-passed law enabled state-owned companies and entities to conceal their contractors, which they immediately did.

If you use the *Forbes* ratings and calculate the state contracts that the "Kings of state contracts" received over 10 years, then the Rotenberg family leaves everyone in the dust. They are the Kings of Kings, with 2,457 trillion rubles in state contracts for merely the 10 years. Among others topping the list are the Jordanian-born StroiGazConsulting founder Ziyad Manasir (843 billion rubles), and entities linked to Putin's old friend Gennady Timchenko (596.5 billion rubles). Timchenko made the State Contract Kings list mainly because of his shares in StroiTransGaz and StroiTransNefteGaz

---

133 Aleksey Stakhanov (1906-1977) was a legendary Hero of Socialist Labor, whose extraordinary mining records were supposed to serve as a model for other workers and to demonstrate the superiority of the socialist system. Workers who set production records were termed "Stakhanovites" in his honor. In the 1980s, various sources disputed the truth of these records, saying that they were staged and he had been helped by other workers.

construction companies, although he had been active in business even before Putin came to power, selling Kirish oil refinery products. In 1997, Timchenko and his partner Torbjörn Törnqvist founded the oil trading company Gunvor, which rather quickly became a major supplier of Russian oil to foreign markets.[134]

Another name on the Kings of State Contracts list is Iskander Makhmudov, known for doing business with the Cherny brothers. Makhmudov had been suspected of ties to the Izmailovo OCG (organized crime group).[135] In 2012, Makhmudov and his partner Andrei Bokarev became Gennady Timchenko's partners, buying 13% of Transoil from Timchenko. Makhmudov's and Bokarev's companies obtained 664.4 billion rubles in Russian state contracts over 10 years.

The Rotenberg family clearly leads by a huge margin, and that is based on only ten-year data. It is mind-boggling how much in state funds the Rotenbergs acquired over the 20 years that Putin has been in power. Arkady Rotenberg started getting seriously involved in business only after Vladimir Putin became president. Back in 1964, Arkady Rotenberg and Putin started judo training together. Arkady and his brother Boris got involved in supplying pipes and quickly started getting all large

---

134 https://www.forbes.ru/profile/gennadii-timchenko?ysclid=lhkcm5s4xw627444078 [in Russian].

135 https://www.svoboda.org/a/doli-v-kompaniyah-rzhd-prodany-biznesmenam-iz-izmaylovskoy-opg/31921878.html [in Russian].

Gazprom contracts, with and without bidding. The Rotenbergs later switched to construction.

Among the large contracts the Rotenberg family was awarded were *Sila Sibiri* (Siberian Strength) pipeline construction and construction of the Crimea bridge, obtaining both contracts without bidding. For a long time, the Rotenberg family's main income source was StroiGazMontazh, which the brothers Arkady and Boris first owned jointly; then Arkady became its sole owner. In March 2020, by Putin's decree, Arkady Rotenberg was awarded the Hero of Labor title.

Mafia state methods: everything is done quietly, in the shadows

The presidential administration buys watches with alligator skin bands. Drummers from Burundi are brought in to a Sakhalin gubernatorial reception. Rosneft buys vodka shot glasses at 11,000 rubles a piece, ice tongs at 35,000 each, a caviar dish for 83,000 rubles, teaspoons at 11,000 each. Luxury at the expense of the state is an everyday occurrence.

If Russia is viewed as a mafia state, the logic behind many Russian government actions becomes clear. The state directly serves the mafia's interests; as Magyar says, "enrichment occurs at the national policy level." In order to hide enrichment at the expense of the state, concealment must be permitted. In late 2017, using Western sanctions as an excuse, the Russian government started allowing companies not to disclose various information. Whereas in the early 2000s, the desire for business transparency and openness prevailed, by the end of twenty years, this "vestige of an infatuation with democracy and Western standards" was abandoned, and money once again fell in love with silence. The more that money landed with the mafia group, the more that silence was needed.

Procurement is a sore subject for all state-owned companies, ministries, departments, and other state entities. Before 2017, mandatory disclosure of bidding documentation on the government procurement website allowed the public to keep track of egregious government spending: luxury cars and furnishings, overpriced souvenirs, services, multi-billion ruble contracts to government-affiliated contractors, etc. In 2017, however, Dmitry Medvedev signed a decree permitting state-owned companies not to disclose information about its suppliers and contractors.[136] Consequently, Gazprom, Transneft, Sberbank, Rosneft, and *Vneshtorgbank* ceased publishing information on bid winners, and much documentation also remained secret. Who gets the multi-million ruble contracts, who are the sole suppliers, what goods or services are procured – all this has been shrouded in secrecy since 2017.

After 2017, state agencies do not disclose such information either: the Ministry of Defense, Federal Protection Service, FSB, The Administrative Directorate of the President of the Russian Federation , the Russian

---

136 http://publication.pravo.gov.ru/Document/View/0001201711290014 [in Russian].

National Guard. The public is thus no longer able to have oversight over government spending.

Two years later, the government again exercised its right to permit concealing information. On April 4, 2019, a new decree was signed, citing 18 instances in which concealing data from the public is permitted.[137] This includes information on deals, affiliated entities, owners, subsidiaries, and contractual partners. None of this has to be openly accessible if the individual or company is under sanctions or under threat of sanctions; if it's a bank involved in state defense contracting; if information pertains to a transaction involving defense contracting or military technical cooperation. And, understandably, the entire mafia group is under sanctions.

Information is concealed not only from the public at large, but even from some minority shareholders, who may be left in the dark about major owners of assets in which the minority shareholders have invested. This restriction in access to information was a "gift" from Vladimir Putin, who signed the relevant decree. Under the Securities Market Law, shareholders holding 1% or more voting shares were able to request information about other shareholders from the registrar keeping the company's shareholder registry, such as shareholder names and the number of shares held. After Putin's decree, however, the registrar no longer has to provide information on individual shareholders if the securities

---

137 http://government.ru/docs/36361/ [in Russian].

issuer has the right to limit information disclosure.[138] After 2022, even more restrictions to information access came into effect.

Another topic of concern to Putin's elites is the access to information about property owners. Information on real estate owners is entered into the Russian State Registry, and eventually the public learns of yet another condo worth billions of rubles owned by state-owned companies' top brass or high-ranking officials' relatives, or the expensive villa that's better described as a palace.

Periodically, attempts are made to classify this information, too. For example, former Prosecutor General Chaika's sons Artem and Igor Chaika were listed in the Russian State Registry of real estate owners first as "LSDUZ" [*sic – gibberish letters – transl.*] and IFYaU9 [*sic – gibberish letters – transl.*], and later were obfuscated altogether under the name "Russian Federation." "Russian Federation" was also the cover for Putin's former deputy prime minister and deputy chief of staff and current head of Rosneft Igor Sechin's real estate holdings. The Russian State Registry also hid information regarding real estate owned by the heads of the FSB and Ministry of Defense, as well by Prime Minister Mikhail Mishustin.[139]

---

138 https://www.vedomosti.ru/finance/articles/2019/08/22/809390-aktsioneram [in Russian].

139 https://openmedia.io/news/n3/rosreestr-spryatal-nedvizhimost-rukovodstva-minoborony-i-fsb-a-takzhe-doma-igorya-sechina-i-mixaila-mishustina/ [in Russian].

Thus, the mafia state hides in the shadows. In contrast to corrupt regimes, where data are concealed in circumvention of the law or using gaps in the law, *in a mafia state, laws are rewritten to accommodate the ruling group's interests, making it possible to conceal assets, income, and property.*

Mafia state methods: using benefits and subsidies

No other company in Russia ever received as many tax breaks as Vladimir Putin approved for Rosneft, led by Igor Sechin. For example, Rosneft received a tax deduction of 46.5 billion rubles annually for 10 years for developing the Priobskoye oilfield.[140] Gazprom Neft, which also developed part of the Priobskoye oilfield, received a tax deduction of 13.5 billion rubles annually, also for 10 years, which means that over the 10 years, the Russian state received 600 billion rubles less. For the Samotlor oilfield, Rosneft received a 10-yr tax deduction totaling 350 billion rubles,[141] justifying the tax break by complex production conditions – high water cut oilfields and hard-to-recover reserves. The question is, why buy such problematic assets? Rosneft got Samotlor with all its Soviet-era problems when Rosneft paid top dollar for TNK-BP. Rosneft itself was largely responsible for the

---

140 https://thebell.io/za-nalogovye-lgoty-dlya-rosnefti-zaplatyat-vse-ostalnye-neftyaniki [in Russian].

141 https://quote.ru/news/article/5ae098102ae5961b67a1a896 [in Russian].

"complications" with the Priobskoye oil deposit. Priobskoye is a main asset of Yuganskneftegaz, which Rosneft acquired through Yukos' bankruptcy. High water cut is not just a natural characteristic, it is also the consequence of active development of the oilfield and using fracking. Because Rosneft production was dropping in a number of large sectors, as soon as state-owned Rosneft acquired Yuganskneftegaz, it started exploiting it most actively. In 2006, the most massive fracking in Russia was done on Priobskoye oilfield using 864 tons of proppant. In 2009, Rosneft reportedly produced 33.8 million tons of oil there, and Priobskoye oilfield productivity increased by 24% over three years. After 10 years of intense development, it is no wonder the oilfield became problematic, repeating Samotlor oilfield's fate.

Rosneft received tax breaks for its Arctic projects, too, even for Rosneft's Vankor cluster, which the government refused to acknowledge as related to the Arctic.[142] Arctic tax breaks were approved on the basis of a list and were granted to various projects, with the main beneficiaries being Rosneft, Novatek, and NefteGazHolding of Sechin's friend Eduard Khudainatov (a former Rosneft president).

Probably the sole Rosneft request for state assistance that was denied is the 2014 Rosneft request to buy 1.5 trillion rubles worth of new Rosneft bonds using National Welfare Fund money.[143] Rosneft was one of the first companies placed under sanctions, and

---

142 https://www.interfax.ru/business/697888 [in Russian].

143 https://www.forbes.ru/news/275531-smi-nazvali-pokupatelei-obligatsii-rosnefti-na-625-mlrd-rublei [in Russian].

it immediately sought help from the National Welfare Fund. Finance Minister Anton Siluanov even disclosed the amount sought: over 2 trillion rubles.[144] Sechin did not receive money from the National Welfare Fund, but Rosneft did place 625 billion rubles in bonds. The largest placement occurred in strict secrecy, in accordance with the "special operation" tradition. The securities were sold to anonymous buyers, and the media later named Vneshtorgbank as the main participant in the placement.[145] After this placement, the ruble exchange rate plummeted,[146] which was explained in part by hard currency purchases in Rosneft's interests, as Rosneft had to pay $7 billion to international creditors and was therefore looking for funds wherever it could. In November 2014, the Central Bank launched hard currency repurchase auctions that enabled banks to bring investment-grade bonds to the Central Bank and use them as security in exchange for hard currency.[147] Rosneft bonds were listed as such securities.

---

144 https://www.forbes.ru/news/271483-rosneft-poprosila-iz-fnb-bolee-2-trln-rublei [in Russian].

145 https://www.forbes.ru/news/275531-smi-nazvali-pokupatelei-obligatsii-rosnefti-na-625-mlrd-rublei [in Russian].

146 https://www.znak.com/2014-12-16/ekonomisty_predstavili_cepochku_kak_rosneft_obrushila_rubl [in Russian].

147 https://yandex.ru/turbo/forbes.ru/s/obshchestvo/375387-sekret-devalvacii-pochemu-v-2014-godu-obvalilsya-rubl [in Russian].

Mafia state methods: creating state corporations

In a mafia state, as the mafia controls both its own business and state-owned business, there is no significant difference in the form of ownership. Nevertheless, Russia created special forms of ownership, such as the rather unique "state corporations." These corporations received hundreds of state-owned enterprises at their disposal, for free. Those state-owned enterprises were now no longer owned by the state, and state corporations were now making decisions about their income on behalf of the state.

Finance Minister Aleksey Kudrin noted: "Transferring <...> stock is essentially intended to divert stock sale proceeds away from the federal budget; the proceeds are supposed to go to the federal budget in accordance with the law "On privatizing state and municipal property."[148] Sergei Chemezov, who headed the state corporation *Rostekhnologii* (Russian Technologies, Rostekh), said: "Now it's not private property and it is not state property. It is the property of a state corporation."[149]

148 https://www.vedomosti.ru/newspaper/articles/2008/07/17/kompaniya-nedeli-rostehnologii [in Russian].

149 https://www.vedomosti.ru/newspaper/articles/2008/07/14/nas-interesuet-mashinostroenie---sergej-chemezov-generalnyj-direktor-goskorporacii-rostehnologii [in Russian].

State corporations now had entire industries at their disposal, as well as access to concessionary loans.

State corporations are established in accordance with the law on non-profit organizations, which means that disclosing profit is not obligatory. The state pumped money into state corporations non-stop, with no regard for the efficiency of such budgetary infusions. For example, between the time it was created in 2007 and 2021, *Rosnano*[150] received 405 billion rubles in state support (including loan guarantees); 132.3 billion of that amount was direct financing.[151] Nevertheless, of Rosnano's top 20 most heavily funded projects, three ended in bankruptcy or were liquidated, and nine others suffered losses, according to the Russian business daily *Vedomosti*.[152]

By forming state corporations, all the conditions were essentially put in place for utilizing state funds in accordance with various interests. *State corporations are symbols of* the *Putin era.*

Putin was actually the main ideologist behind creating state corporations *en* masse. Out of eight state cor-

---

150 A state-established joint stock company designed to develop a competitive nanotechnology industry in Russia.

151 https://www.vedomosti.ru/economics/articles/2021/11/25/897477-rosnano-gospomoschi-dolgi?ysclid=lhlsas5ol8806758726 [in Russian].

152 https://www.vedomosti.ru/economics/articles/2021/11/25/897477-rosnano-gospomoschi-dolgi?ysclid=lhlsas5ol8806758726 [in Russian].

porations created in Russia, six were formed on Putin's initiative or with his active assistance. He personally proposed the creation of the two largest state corporations – *Rosatom* and *Rostekhnologiya* – to the State Duma (bypassing the government).[153] The president also personally appointed heads of most state corporations. Putin's friend and colleague at the KGB and in Dresden, *Rostekh* state corporation head Sergei Chemezov described Putin's role: "If it weren't for his directive, I think we'd still be trying to get signed approval from all the departments."[154]

As head of *Rostekh*, Chemezov was awarded the Hero of Russia star by secret decree, and even if you only count his official income, it exceeded one billion rubles. While average Russians lost income when the ruble exchange rate fell, "insiders'" losses were compensated with higher salaries. For example, Chemezov's annual income increased five-fold: from 62.5 million rubles in 2012 to 332.8 million rubles in 2018.

All six of Putin's state corporations – *Olimpstroi* (Olympic Construction) *Bank Razvitiya* (Development Bank", later RF *Vneshekonombank* RF), *Rosnanotekh* (later Rosnano), Housing Restructuring Assistance Fund, *Rostekhnologii* (Russian Technologies, later Rostekh) and *Rosatom* were created in late 2007, during the last few

---

153 https://www.kommersant.ru/doc/1260785 [in Russian].

154 https://www.vedomosti.ru/newspaper/articles/2008/07/14/nas-interesuet-mashinostroenie---sergej-chemezov-generalnyj-direktor-goskorporacii-rostehnologii [in Russian].

months of Putin's second presidential term. All these state corporations received assets and funds. Over 600 billion rubles were allocated to capitalize these state corporations in 2007 alone.[155]

State corporations, their subsidiaries and affiliated companies award contracts to companies and organizations linked to the mafia circle *persons or their relatives*. For example, NIR fund received funding through Rosatom and its subsidiaries. NIR is headed by Katerina Tikhonova, Vladimir Putin's reputed daughter. In 2016-2019, NIR Fund received 355.5 million rubles in contracts from *AtomEnergoProm* JSC.

Mafia state methods: state-owned companies for "insiders"

Practically all of the largest state-controlled JSCs (joint-stock companies) are headed by Putin's friends and cronies. Rosneft is headed by Igor Sechin, Gazprom – by Aleksey Miller, Gazprom Neft – by Aleksandr Dyukov, Transneft – by Nikolai Tokarev (Putin's KGB colleague), *Sberbank* – by German Gref, *Aeroflot* was headed for many years by Vitaly Savelyev (who chaired the Russia Bank management board in 1993). *Sovkomflot'* longtime head was Sergei Frank, whose son Gleb married Gennady Timchenko's daughter Ksenia. For years, Russian Railroads was headed by Vladimir Yakunin, who co-founded the *Ozero* cooperative. The world's largest

---

155 https://www.vedomosti.ru/economics/articles/2019/10/08/813068-20-let-stagnatsii [in Russian].

diamond producer *Alrosa*'s general manager was Sergei Ivanov, son of the former presidential administration head and Putin's KGB coworker [also named] Sergei Ivanov. *RosSelkhozBank* was managed for eight years by Dmitry Patrushev, the son of Security Council secretary Nikolai Patrushev.

The state manages companies through its representatives on boards of directors. Government officials are not remunerated for this work, but other members of boards of directors receive significant amounts. This forms an additional (and very significant) source of income for "insiders" – not just close associates but also former government officials *and foreigners who are or have been "useful."* For example, *Gazprom Neft* board of directors' members, aside from Miller, are former *Gazprom Export* general manager Aleksandr Medvedev, former head of *Gazprom MezhRegionGaz* Kirill Seleznev, and former Leningrad Region governor Valery Serdyukov. In 2015, the *Rostelekom* board of directors' chairman was replaced by former presidential administration head Sergei Ivanov, who became the president's special representative on nature protection, the environment and transport issues. *Rostelekom's* board of directors includes *Vneshtorgbank* head Andrei Kostin, *Sogaz* chairman of the management board Anton Ustinov, and head of the *Talant i Uspekh* (Talent and Success) Fund (founded by the cellist Roldugin) Yelena Shmeleva. A seat on the *Rostelekom* board of directors comes with an annual salary of two million rubles, with the chairman receiving more.

Russian Direct Investment Fund general manager Kirill Dmitriev merits special note. Dmitriev managed to join the narrow circle and become an insider. At one time, Dmitriev was called the informal liaison between the Kremlin and Donald Trump's team.[156] Dmitriev's wife Natalya Popova is a deputy for Putin's reputed daughter Katerina Tikhonova; they attended MGU (Moscow State University) together. Dmitriev is on the boards of directors of *Rostelekom, Transneft*, Russian Railroads, as well as on the *Alrosa* supervisory board.

Mikhail Kovalchuk – president of Kurchatov Institute and Yuri Kovalchuk's brother, unexpectedly joined Sberbank's supervisory board.

Prior to the February 2022 full-scale invasion of Ukraine, Putin's longtime acquaintance Matthias Warnig, former *Stasi* officer and former head of Russian Dresdner Bank, sat on the boards of directors of *Rosneft* and *Transneft* and on *Vneshtorgbank*'s supervisory board. Warnig was termed one of the highest-paid independent foreign directors in Russia and a channel for informing Putin about the most important companies and industries.[157] After Russia's full-scale invasion of Ukraine, Warnig was forced to resign from all boards of directors under public pressure in Germany.

Being on multiple boards of directors enables "enforcers" from different clans to monitor each other

---

156 https://thebell.io/drug-docheri-putina-i-bankir-s-10-mlrd-chto-my-znaem-o-kirille-dmitrieve-kotorogo-nazvali-cvyaznym-mezhdu-kremlem-i-trampom [in Russian].

157 https://www.forbes.ru/sobytiya/vlast/103069-kak-chekist-iz-gdr-stal-samym-nadezhnym-ekonomistom-putina-rassledovanie-forbe [in Russian].

and earn additional income. And it's a way for Putin to obtain information and informers' reports from various sources.

Mafia state methods: unofficial ways of getting close

In a mafia state, unofficial organizations play a special role. In Russia, these include the Russian Geographic Society, Night Hockey League, *Zenit* soccer club, Mountain Hunters' Club, Russian Equestrian Federation, and some others.

Vladimir Putin himself chairs the Russian Geographic Society's supervisory board, and the society's president is Defense Minister Sergei Shoigu. The society's supervisory board boasts representatives from Russia's biggest companies; before the war with Ukraine, several foreigners were also on the board: BP group of companies' chief executive director Bernard Looney, Alibaba Group partner Jack Ma, and chairman of Ferring Pharmaceuticals LLC board of directors Frederik Dag Arfst Paulsen. Not only Putin and Shoigu represent the Russian government at the Geographic Society but also presidential administration head Anton Vaino, his first deputy Aleksey Gromov, Putin's press secretary Dmitry Peskov, former administration head Sergei Ivanov, Foreign Minister Sergei Lavrov, Federation Council Chairperson Valentina Matvienko, and Moscow Mayor Sergei Sobyanin. Business circles give money and grants to the Geographic Society in a display of loyalty to the regime's ideas and wishes. Attending regular sessions of the Geographic Society's supervisory board is an opportunity for business people to participate in less formal, more private meetings than, for example, Putin's get-togethers with the Russian Union of Industrialists and Entrepreneurs.[158]

Night Hockey League games are another opportunity to establish informal ties with the circle surrounding the mafia, and if you get lucky, you can honorably lose to Vladimir Putin in the hopes that later on the loss will pay off. The amateur Russian national hockey championship "Night Hockey League" was founded in 2011 on Putin's initiative. Putin himself regularly plays in the league's gala match. Incredibly, having first put on ice skates at 60, Putin manages to score several goals during a game. Several businessmen took part in gala matches: Timchenko, Boris Rotenberg, Vladimir Potanin, and Dmitry Bosov (Bosov committed suicide in 2020). Training sessions, games, and the locker room are extremely comfortable venues for staying in touch. Actually, you don't even have to play hockey; you can just attend the games and profess your love for the sport.

Mafia state methods: illegal business

In a mafia state, the ruling clan is either involved in illegal business both domestically and abroad, or else it operates a protection racket for an illegal business by shielding it from prosecution.

---

158 Under US sanctions since August 2023, https://home.treasury.gov/news/press-releases/jy1690.

In 2018, a glaring example attracted the world's attention. Argentina's Defense Minister Patricia Bullrich posted on *Twitter* videos of almost 400 kg. of cocaine being seized from the Russian Embassy in Buenos Aires. Officially, it was stated that this was a joint operation of Argentinian and Russian law enforcement. Suitcases of cocaine at the embassy were discovered in November 2016, and, in December 2017, in a special FSB operation, the suitcases were delivered to Moscow on Security Council secretary Nikolai Patrushev's charter flight. It was announced that the 12 suitcases of cocaine belonged to mysterious Russian citizen Andrei Kovalchuk, who became the main defendant in the case. Experts and investigators in Russia and Argentina interviewed by Dossier Center agreed: Russian and Argentinean intelligence and law enforcement agencies may have colluded in order to downplay the incident's political significance, avoid a complicated and full analysis of all aspects of the case, and to conceal the possible role high-ranking Russian and Argentinean officials played in drug smuggling.[159] The drug trade, illegal weapons trade, illegal prostitution, and illegal gambling are the mafia's traditional criminal activities all over the world. In a mafia state, all this activity remains outside the law but often has patrons from the state, primarily from law enforcement.

Russia is an important link in the global drug trafficking chain. Approximately 30% of the world's heroin passes through Central Asia and on to Europe, China,

---

159 https://cocaina.dossier.center/part1/ [in Russian].

and beyond.[160] In 2010, the UN labeled Russia a world leader in heroin shipments; at the time, the EU and the RF consumed almost half of all heroin produced. According to a UN report for 2018, Russia still holds first place in Eastern Europe and is still an important world market for sales and distribution. Although synthetic drugs are gaining popularity, around 70 tons of opioids are shipped from Afghanistan to Russia each year. Russia receives 21% of all heroin produced in the world, and 5% of all opiates.[161]

The largest organized crime groups such as Solntsevo and Tambov mobs engage in drug trafficking.Local gangs can certainly be used to handle large drug shipments, but it is more efficient to work with corrupt government officials and businessmen who are able to arrange the transport.

Afghanistan produces around 84% of the world's opium; Iran is another large producer and transit point. The UN report notes that contraband groups started using this route: transporting heroin in trucks across Iran to Central Asian countries, then to Customs Union countries, including Kyrgyzstan, Kazakhstan, Russia, and Belarus, and on to the final destinations in Western

---

160 https://secretmag.ru/stories/rossiya-potreblyaet-20-mirovogo-geroina-vot-kak-ustroen-narkoticheskii-rynok-segodnya.htm [in Russian].

161 https://secretmag.ru/stories/rossiya-potreblyaet-20-mirovogo-geroina-vot-kak-ustroen-narkoticheskii-rynok-segodnya.htm

and Central Europe.[162] Obviously, the process was interrupted in February 2022.

Narcotics sales in Russia are estimated at around $60 billion annually.[163] This huge market could not exist without powerful patrons and curators in the ruling entities. For example, in 2021, a former Russian Federal Drug Control Service for Moscow and Moscow Region department head was arrested on suspicion of establishing a network of underground drug-manufacturing laboratories and running this business. Experts are convinced that it would be impossible to engage in such activity without high-ranking patrons.[164]

The media stated that one of the "curators" of the illegal drug trade in Russia was Putin's associate and former KGB officer Viktor Ivanov. Ivanov had long been officially involved with narcotics as head of the Federal Drug Control Service (disbanded in 2016). A year before the Federal Drug Control Service was disbanded, London's High Court published material concerning the murder of former FSB officer Aleksandr Litvinenko in London. The materials included a confidential file on Viktor Ivanov compiled for the British company Titon by former KGB colonel Yuri Shvetz in September 2006 at Aleksandr Litvinenko's request. According to former Titon head Dean Attew's statements during an open

---

162 https://wdr.unodc.org/wdr2020/field/WDR20_Booklet_3.pdf.

163 https://life.ru/p/860938 [in Russian].

164 https://360tv.ru/tekst/obschestvo/imperija-veschestv/ [in Russian].

inquiry at London's High Court, Litvinenko may have been killed because of this file, which contained compromising information on Ivanov and was responsible for Ivanov's losing out on a multi-billion government contract for which he had been lobbying. According to the dossier, Viktor Ivanov cooperated closely with head of the Tambov organized crime group Vladimir Kumarin, who helped Ivanov establish control over the St. Petersburg seaport, which was then used to smuggle drugs from Colombia to Europe.[165]

For a long time, the gaming business was legal in Russia, but it became illegal on July 1, 2009, with the exception of five specially organized gaming zones. This does not mean the gaming business disappeared. As often happens in such cases when some pointless prohibition is introduced, gambling went underground but under the protection of the power agencies. Previously, according to media information, even legal casinos in several regions, such as the Moscow Region, were under the protection of the prosecutor's office.[166] After the prohibition, the popular *Vulkan* (Volcano) casino chain continued operating in Moscow and the Moscow Region under the prosecutors' supervision, with the prosecutors being monitored by the

---

165 https://www.bbc.com/russian/rolling_news/2015/04/150430_rn_litvinenko_ivanov_report_published [in Russian].

166 https://www.kommersant.ru/doc/1892981 [in Russian].

FSB.[167] In 2011, there was a scandal: the FSB announced that illegal gaming halls were discovered in 15 Moscow Region cities. A link was revealed between the Moscow Region prosecutorial leadership and staff and underground gaming business representatives. According to the FSB: "In particular, close ties existed between illegal gaming business head Ivan Nazarov and Moscow Region First Deputy Prosecutor Aleksandr Ignatenko, several prosecutors from Moscow Region entities and heads of structural divisions of the Prosecutor's Office, and the Moscow Region Main Internal Affairs Administration."[168] The Moscow Region prosecutors' case was the most famous, but there are regular reports, mostly from the FSB, about police officers or prosecutorial staff patronizing underground gaming businesses in various Russian regions. Rather than an indication of a campaign against illegal casinos, this more likely indicates that various law enforcement clans are fighting among themselves for the right to patronize the casinos.

Mafia clans around the world traditionally engage in the illegal arms trade. In 2008, Russian citizen Viktor Bout was detained in Bangkok at the request of the U.S.; the U.S. had charged Bout with illegally shipping arms to Colombia's Revolutionary Armed Forces [FARC], which the U.S. regards as a terrorist organization. Bout was extradited to the U.S., convicted in 2012, and sentenced to 25 years in prison. Former U.S. State Department official and Stratfor agency VP of the tac-

---

167 https://iz.ru/news/503685 [in Russian].

168 https://www.interfax.ru/russia/177923 [in Russian].

tical intelligence department Scott Stewart believes that the airline company that Bout owned was a good cover for arms dealing, i.e., the planes were needed for the arms trade itself and for masking the arms trade. Stewart speculated that Bout could not do what he did without the knowledge of someone high in the Russian vertical of power or without at least the approval from above, especially if you look at the scope of his activity. According to Stewart, practically all large countries have "their own" arms dealers with whom they secretly work in one way or another in order to advance the countries' interests in certain regions of the world. For example, it was learned that one of Bout's first operations was arming the forces opposing the Taliban in Afghanistan, which essentially accorded with Russia's interests in the region.[169]

On December 8, 2022, as part of official talks between Russia and the U.S., Viktor Bout was exchanged for U.S. Olympian basketball star Brittney Griner. Griner had been convicted in Russia for drug possession; she had transported vape cartridges containing less than a gram of hashish oil. She had received the prescription for the medical cannabis, illegal in Russia, from her doctor in the U.S.

Viktor Bout's return to Russia was widely covered on all Russian TV channels, which tracked literally every step of this process, turning it into a touching TV series

---

169 https://www.bbc.com/russian/international/2010/08/100824_interview_us_bout [in Russian].

for the viewer, "a hero returning from enemy captivity." Propagandists presented this as Russia's following the principle "leave no man behind." This principle, however, does not apply to everybody, only to those who are valuable to the mafia clan, whom the mafia clan needs, who performs its tasks, or who was valuable in the past and deserves recognition for services rendered. By contrast, the propaganda channels never covered any prisoner exchange during the war with Ukraine so broadly and so triumphantly.

Russia's foreign policy

The mafia state's main principle is that everything is done in the mafia group's interests, in both domestic policy and economy and in foreign policy too. Collaborating and partnering with the West, peaceful co-existence with neighbors would benefit Russia as a state, but *it is not in line with the ruling group's goals.*

The annexation of Crimea in 2014 was followed by military action in eastern Ukraine, and the culmination was the 2022 full-scale invasion. This was not surprising, however; on the contrary, it fell in line with the overall foreign policy characteristic of the mafia state. The events themselves sent the clear message that *it is a no-rules game from now on.*

Over the entire 20 years of Putin's rule, Putin's "elites" visibly wanted to utilize the West for their interests while simultaneously they were unwilling to accept Western society's principles and rules. Putin's circle preferred to keep their money, educate their children, and acquire real estate and assets in the West while adhering to the authoritarian *mafiosi* system in Russia and advancing its practices outside of Russia.

Mafia state methods: seeking an external enemy

Over the past 20 years, the concept of a "besieged fortress" became firmly ingrained in Russia. All these years, the regime worked at convincing citizens of the existence of an external enemy, which facilitated mobilizing people around the regime, ramping up the law enforcement bloc, and explaining and justifying authoritarian governance methods. When Putin came to power, the enemy was terrorism, which enabled joint counter-terrorism efforts with the West. The differences in values between the mafia state and democratic nations, however, were too great. After all, terrorism is much less of a threat to authoritarian rule than is democracy, which requires honest elections and alternation of leadership. The *West, therefore, was more suitable for the role of the external enemy*. Automatically, democratic values thus became hostile values, and discrediting them became important to assuring the mafia regime's survival. An anti-democratic bloc started forming around Russia as a mafia state, with focal points of influence not just in other authoritarian states but also within democratic countries, too, thus ensuring the advancement of Vladimir Putin's and his clan's interests from within.

Actually, this was probably more the case before the February full-scale invasion of Ukraine. After the full-scale invasion started, essentially all Russia's opportunities to influence politicians or businesses in democratic countries were eliminated. Russia itself became much more dependent on China (and Iran, too) and does not seem to be the nucleus around which a world that is an alternative to the West is forming.

Mafia state methods: guarantees to "insiders"

When Israel Prime Minister and Vladimir Putin's good friend Benjamin Netanyahu lost his post, jokes were popular in both countries about Netanyahu's place in the line of former politicians wanting to become members of the Gazprom board of directors. Netanyahu preferred to stay in Israel and continue to be active in politics. But jokes do not arise without reason. In conveyor mode, retired politicians from democratic countries received high positions in Russian state companies (and some private companies) – naturally, if they had previously adhered to pro-Russian policies. This changed only after the full-scale invasion of Ukraine.

On June 29, 2020, a Paris criminal court convicted former French premier François Fillon and sentenced him to five years in prison (three of those years as a suspended sentence) for embezzling state funds. Fillon was also barred from holding governmental positions. He was accused of hiring his wife as an assistant while holding various government posts himself. The investigators determined that Fillon's wife did not fulfill her responsibilities, but she received top salaries, costing the French state over one million Euro. Exactly one year after the verdict, the former French premier was appointed to the board of directors of the *Zarubezhneft* state-owned company by a Russian governmental decree. *Zarubezhneft's* website says that the company is a conduit for state interests in the area of fuel and energy on the world arena (of course, meaning Russian state interests). Fillon now had a new boss: chairman of

Zarubezhneft board of directors Evgeny Murov, formerly with the KGB and the FSB, who headed the Federal Protection Service for 16 years under Putin. The warm ties between Putin and Fillon started when both were Prime Ministers (2008-2012). For example, in spring 2008, Prime Minister Fillon was the first Western leader openly to speak out against presenting Ukraine and Georgia with the Action Plan to join NATO.[170]

The starkest and most prominent example of profitable "job placement" of a Western politician in Russia is that of former German Chancellor Gerhard Schröder, who chaired the Rosneft board of directors since 2017 in partnership with Igor Sechin (with Sechin modestly taking the spot of Schröder's deputy on the board of directors). Schröder also headed the shareholders' committee of Nord Stream AG, created in order to manage the Nord Stream pipeline. At Rosneft, Schröder was entitled to remuneration of $600,000 a year. Schröder rejected the remuneration,[171] but Rosneft insisted,[172] and since then, the state-owned Rosneft reports show that the former German chancellor was paid $600,000 for 2017, $600,000 for 2018, and the same amount for 2019. People in Germany were skeptical of Schröder's position at Rosneft (and after February 2022, the attitude became

---

170 https://novayagazeta.ru/articles/2017/03/23/71879-teper-u-fiyona-trudnosti-s-putinym?ysclid=lhrjmxgmvo105987774 [in Russian].

171 https://www.vedomosti.ru/business/articles/2018/01/22/748590-shreder [in Russian].

172 https://www.kommersant.ru/doc/3528701 [in Russian].

highly negative), but this did not stop the former chancellor from advocating improving ties with the Russian government, including the need to support the proRussian position on the Kremlin's most controversial issues. In an interview with the German publication *Tagesspiegel* in early May 2020, Schröder called for lifting the sanctions against Russia, saying in effect that Germany did not value highly enough the fact that Russia, despite the terrible past was ready trustingly to collaborate with the new Germany: "It is not appropriate for us to continue supporting sanctions against Russia. First, they evoke historic memories in Russia; second, they do not change Russian policies. Especially now, when we are beginning to experience economic difficulties are because of the Corona crisis, we need greater cooperation. That's why the pointless sanctions must be lifted. Whoever thinks Russia can be forced to do anything using sanctions, is mistaken. No Russian president is ever going to give Crimea back to Ukraine. That's reality."[173] The former German chancellor and the Russian president are longtime friends. Even after the war in Ukraine started, Schröder continued traveling to Russia and meeting with Putin, despite being forced to leave the Rosneft Board of Directors under public pressure in Germany.

Also worth recalling is the former Austrian Foreign Minister Karin Kneissl (who held that post December 2017 – June 2019). Kneissl gained notoriety when Vladi-

---

173 https://www.tagesspiegel.de/politik/altkanzler-schroeder-im-interview-die-unsinnigen-russland-sanktionen-muessen-weg/25795514.html [in German].

mir Putin, a guest at her wedding in 2018, raised a toast and danced with the bride. In June 2021, Kneissl, too, joined the Rosneft Board of Directors and made numerous public statements against Russian sanctions. After the war in Ukraine started, Kneissl, facing possible personal sanctions, left the Rosneft Board of Directors, and even left Austria. In summer 2023, she spent time in Russia's Petrushevo Village in Ryazan Region.[174]

Just as people questioned the actions of Germany's Schröder, questions also arose regarding former Finnish Prime Minister Esko Tapani Aho, who was on *Sberbank*'s supervisory council together with, for example, Mikhail Kovalchuk. In the 1980s, Esko Tapani Aho was a member of the Finnish parliament, then chairman of the Finnish Center party. He was prime minister starting April 26, 1991, and in that position he actively supported collaborating with Russia and building partnerships with Russia's border regions. He visited Russia several times, including visits to Karelia (1992), St. Petersburg and Leningrad Region (1993), and Murmansk Region (1994).[175] During those years, he met Sobchak and Chubais. Esko Tapani Aho simultaneously held five positions involving Russia in one way or another. For example, he was chairman of the Finnish-Russian Chamber of Commerce, board member at Skolkovo scientific and research center, and lecturer at the Russian Academy of the National Economy.

---

174 https://tass.ru/obschestvo/18520021 [in Russian].

175 https://ru.wikipedia.org/wiki/%D0%90%D1%85%D0%BE,_%D0%AD%D1%81%D0%BA%D0%BE [in Russian].

Since 2014, *Sberbank* has been on the EU and US sanctions lists, yet Esko Tapani Aho continued to work at this essentially Russian state-owned outfit, and he was getting paid good money. According to *Ilta-Sanomat* newspaper, he made around 116,000 Euro from his Sberbank position alone in 2016. In 2017, he received a total of around 330,000 Euro, including salary and return on capital.[176]

All the above-noted politicians have informal ties with Vladimir Putin, conduct foreign policies in pursuit of closer ties with Russia, and, after leaving office, speak out against anti-Russian sanctions.

In 2015, Vladimir Putin signed a decree granting RF citizenship to Italian-born Angelo Codignoni.[177] Since 2011, Codignoni has been on CTC-Media's board of directors, where he represented Mikhail Kovalchuk's interests. Codignoni's biography is notable. Angelo Codignoni co-founded the Italian political party *Forza Italia*, and he was its secretary general in 1993-1994. Another leader and co-founder of this party was former Italian prime minister Silvio Berlusconi, for whom Codignoni had worked as an advisor. Angelo Codignoni was mentioned in U.S. wires posted on WikiLeaks, where he as was referred to as the "liaison" between Berlusconi and the Kremlin.[178] It is doubtful that we will

---

176 https://inosmi.ru/social/20181209/244182740.html [in Russian].

177 https://tass.ru/obschestvo/1770753 [in Russian].

178 https://www.kommersant.ru/doc/1757171 [in Russian],

learn more about the relationships between Codignoni, Berlusconi, and Putin's associates: Codignoni died in 2021, and Berlusconi died in 2023.

Starting in May 2019, Cesare Maria Ragaglini served as deputy chairman of VEB.RF (formerly *Vneshekonombank*).[179] His biography is also very interesting. In 2004-2006, he was Italian Prime Minister Berlusconi's representative regarding G-8 summit issues. For four years, Ragaglini was Italy's permanent representative to the UN in New York. His last diplomatic post in 2013-2017 was as Extraordinary and Plenipotentiary Italian Ambassador in Moscow. Ragaglini was awarded the Order of Friendship by Russian President Vladimir Putin's decree.[180] Clearly, Ragaglini was instrumental in Moscow's cooperation with Rome on numerous issues.

Mafia state methods: creating channels of influence

When the mafia is strong, it replaces the government, which means it operates in symbiosis with a controllable bureaucracy. As the mafia state's interests extend beyond its own country, it also needs "its own" politicians at the international level. The mafia needs politicians who will support and implement its interests. At the mafia state level, this problem has been solved in full: the state apparatus is fully absorbed by the mafia

---

179 https://xn--90ab5f.xn--p1ai/o-banke/#leadership [in Russian],

180 https://www.interfax.ru/business/662384 [in Russian].

and forms an integral part. Solving this problem internationally entails mafia diplomacy.

In seeking to fulfill all its needs, the mafia state creates pockets of influence in other countries. The list of needs includes interests that healthy nations also have – ensuring security and economic cooperation, but the mafia state pursues these using methods that are not so wholesome. Nor are interests in these areas so wholesome either, and sometimes corrupt practices blatantly spread beyond the mafia's own territory. This process has the additional purpose of discrediting democracy.

Throughout Vladimir Putin's rule, the Kremlin directly supported opposition politicians and even entire parties in Western countries. They include: Italy's Northern League leader and Internal Affairs Minister in 2018-2019 Matteo Salvini; head of the French National Rally (formerly National Front) Marine Le Pen; head of the Dutch Party for Freedom Geert Wilders; and cochairman of Alternative for Germany Jörg Meuthen. These politicians have a lot in common: they act as allies during European elections, as a right-wing alliance against the EU. And they support Russian President Vladimir Putin, or at least they did until February 2022.

Head of the French National Rally Party Marine Le Pen openly met with Putin, supported Russia's annexation of Crimea, and opposed imposing European sanctions on Russia. Several years ago, because of its racist and antisemitic past, the National Front had trouble obtaining funding from French banks; Le Pen thus had to look for other funding sources. In 2014, the National

Front received loans from Russian banks in the amount of 11 million Euro. One of the loans, for 9 million Euro, was extended by the small First Czech-Russian Bank, which had ties to the Kremlin.[181] The money was needed for the upcoming French election campaign on the departmental and then regional level.[182] Shortly before obtaining the loan, in spring 2014, the National Front leadership supported Russia's annexation of Crimea. In May 2023, Marine Le Pen once again called Crimea a legitimate part of Russia.[183]

In Austria, suspected ties with Russia caused a big scandal. For over 10 years, Heinz-Christian Strache had been head of the Austrian Freedom Party and also served in the cabinet of Chancellor Sebastian Kurz. In 2019, Strache was forced to resign after the German publications *Der Spiegel* and *Süddeutsche Zeitung* published a video from a villa in Ibiza showing Strache with an acquaintance of his and a young lady described as a "Russian oligarch's niece" discussing the possibility of using cash bribes in Austria, including to the *Kronen*

---

181 https://www.bbc.com/russian/features-39556300 [in Russian].

182 https://www.bbc.com/russian/international/2014/11/141124_russia_front_national_loan_france [in Russian].

183 https://iz.ru/1517778/2023-05-24/marin-le-pen-nazvala-krym-legitimnoi-chastiu-rossii?ysclid=libktb55tv73918263 [in Russian].

Zeitung publication, in order to influence public opinion to shift toward the Austrian Freedom Party.[184]

In Germany, ties with Russia were noted among members of the right-wing Alternative for Germany party. Markus Frohnmaier headed Alternative for Germany's youth organization, served as the party's press secretary, and was later a member of the Bundestag. At one point, Frohnmaier planned a youth cooperation agreement with United Russia.[185] *Focus* magazine noted[186] that another politician, Heinrich Groth, worked for a party subdivision and organized demonstrations related to the "Lisa incident" – a fake story about a Russian girl being raped in Germany made up by the Russian propagandist media. Notably, Alternative for Germany got the most votes in Germany's Eastern regions, in the former German Democratic Republic.

In February 2018, a delegation of European politicians traveled to Crimea. Among them were Alternative for Germany party members from the regional

---

184 https://www.spiegel.de/politik/heinz-christian-strache-fpoe-ist-oesterreichs-vizekanzler-kaeuflich-a-00000000-0002-0001-0000-000163955864 [in German].

185 https://www.dw.com/de/f%C3%BCr-die-afd-ist-russland-ein-gewinnerthema/a-48803982 [in German].

186 https://www.focus.de/politik/deutschland/afd-haelt-namen-ihrer-mitarbeiter-geheim-strippenzieher-mit-verbindung-zur-extremen-rechten-das-sind-die-radikalen-afd-hintermaenner_id_8647802.html [in German].

parliaments of Berlin, Brandenburg, and Rhein-Westphalia. *Der Spiegel* magazine said that the Alternative for Germany party was a lucky find for Vladimir Putin. Their mutual goal – to attack the European establishment – unifies the party with the Russian president, who wants to break the West's power by trying to splinter it. In addition, Alternative for Germany and the Kremlin are ardently anti-American and despise modern Western values.[187]

After the annexation of Crimea, European politicians' visits to the Crimean Peninsula became one of the main instruments of legitimizing the annexation. In July 2015, a group of French National Assembly members headed by French-Russian Dialogue Association co-chairman Thierry Mariani visited Crimea. This event was called a diplomatic breakthrough as it was the first official visit by a European delegation to Crimea and Sevastopol after the Russian annexation.

In September 2015, former Italian premier Silvio Berlusconi visited Crimea privately and met with Vladimir Putin there.[188]

In October 2016, an 18-member delegation consisting of Italian parliament members and businessmen from five regions of Italy (Veneto, Liguria, Lombardy,

187 https://www.spiegel.de/politik/wie-putin-die-afd-fuer-seine-zwecke-missbraucht-a-00000000-0002-0001-0000-000163279501 [in German].

188 https://crimea-news.com/politics/2018/02/05/371980.html [in Russian].

Tuscany, Emilia-Romagna) visited Crimea. From the Italian side, the trip was organized by Venetian parliament member Stefano Valdegamberi, who had called for lifting antiRussian sanctions regionally in Italy: in May 2016, the council of Italy's Veneto region (Venice) adopted a resolution calling on the national government to condemn the EU's policy regarding Crimea and to call for lifting the antiRussian sanctions. However, the Italian senate did not pass this resolution.[189]

In March 2017, a delegation that included members of the European Parliament, politicians from EU nations, CIS countries and Latin America visited Crimea. After the visit, Richard Wood, a member of the UK Independence Party (UKIP) told Russian state news agency *RIA Novosti*: that he had wanted to see the situation in Crimea, and he was absolutely thrilled. He claimed that people wanted to be part of the Russian Federation, and he said that he never heard anyone say that they were being oppressed or that anyone had trouble with the Russian authorities. The West, he asserted, has been long adhering to a very shortsighted policy regarding Russia. He claimed that when he was in Crimea, he didn't see police officers on the street, or soldiers or public unrest, nothing like that.[190] He called for lifting the anti-Russian sanctions. Another UKIP member, Nigel Sussman, who also visited Crimea, told *RIA Novosti* that he intended to write

---

189 https://crimea-news.com/politics/2018/02/05/371980.html [in Russian].

190 https://crimea.ria.ru/society/20170331/1109771642.html [in Russian translation; the English was not available].

an open letter to then-British Prime Minister Theresa May calling for lifting anti-Russian sanctions.[191] All Russian state media covered that visit in detail.[192] UKIP is a right-centrist party that supported Brexit. Another delegation member was Serbian parliamentary deputy Milovan Bojić, who called for lifting the anti-Russian sanctions, as well as Serbian radical party presidium member Aleksandar Šešelj, and Serbian political scientist Srđa Trifković.[193] The Serbian radical party is a nationalist organization[194] that opposes closer relations between Serbia and the EU and advocates Serbia's territorial integrity and Belgrade's close cooperation with Moscow and Beijing.

Another European politician, possibly the closest to Vladimir Putin in spirit, is the Hungarian Prime Minister Victor Orbán, who is also the central figure of his own mafia state, according to Bálint Magyar. It's no accident that Orbán often sides with Russia. After the war in Ukraine started and new sanctions were imposed on Russia, Hungary's position often differed from that of other EU countries. Orbán was able

---

191 https://crimea.ria.ru/society/20170331/1109771642.html [in Russian].

192 https://www.1tv.ru/news/2017-03-20/321919-delegatsiya_evropeyskih_politikov_posetila_krym [in Russian].

193 https://inosmi.ru/politic/20170321/238919299.html [in Russian].

194 https://en.wikipedia.org/wiki/Serbian_Radical_Party [in Russian].

to secure additional gas shipments from Putin at the same time that deliveries of Russian gas to other countries were dropping.

Naturally, there were "insider" politicians in Ukraine, too. Kremlin interests were being pushed by head of *Oppozitsionnaia platforma-Za zhizn'* (Opposition Platform – For Life) party, *Verkhovna Rada* (Ukrainian Parliament) member Viktor Medvedchuk. In 2004, Vladimir Putin and Dmitry Medvedev's wife Svetlana baptized Medvedchuk's daughter Darya at St. Petersburg's Kazan Cathedral. Putin thus became Medvedchuk's daughter's godfather. During Euromaidan (November 2013 - February 2014), then-President Viktor Yanukovych phoned Medvedchuk 54 times, suggesting that Medvedchuk was the main communication channel with Moscow. Medvedchuk- owned media (until the media outlets shut down) promoted pro-Russian ideas.

In October 2021, Medvedchuk was charged [in Ukraine] with treason and abetting terrorist organizations. He was suspected of implementing "a criminal scheme of shipping coal products" from the self-proclaimed People's Republic of Donetsk and the People's Republic of Luhansk from late 2014 to early 2015 and reporting to the Russian government regarding the shipments.

When the war in Ukraine started, Medvedchuk was able to flee, but later he was apprehended by the Ukrainian Security Service, which claimed that Medvedchuk's escape was planned by the FSB, which was supposed to transport him secretly to Russia. In September 2022, Medvedchuk was handed over to Russia in exchange for a group of Ukrainian prisoners of war from the Azov battalion. Medvedchuk was soon stripped of Ukrainian citizenship.

Medvedchuk was actually one of the people instrumental in Putin's decision to invade Ukraine in February 2022, as Medvedchuk had repeatedly told the Russian president about the great support in Ukraine for Putin personally and for Russia in general.[195]

Mafia state methods: interfering in elections

The Washington Post identified two waves of Russian interference from the early 1990s,. The first wave lasted until 2014 and related to former Soviet countries; the second wave started after 2014, spreading significantly to Western countries with stable democracies.

What goals was Russia pursuing when interfering in other countries' domestic affairs? The political goal was clear – to ensure the election of pro-Russian candidates. This would help lower the risk of new sanctions, minimize the probability of investigations of crimes committed by Vladimir Putin's regime and his close associates; ensure the safety of Putin's associates' property and investments abroad (an improbable goal after February 2022); increase the number of supporters of the annexation of Crimea; gain international supporters of Moscow's initiatives; and minimize the harsh international condemnation of repressions and human rights

---

195 https://verstka.media/kak-putin-pridumal-voynu?fbclid=IwAR28XLQAkRtTkrpCbg_-xdY4YBN7eRn4pbbH-7wOjK-R-NTbm3_y-aEXMr6c [in Russian].

violations in Russia. Further goals are destroying democratic institutions and organizations (for example, the European Union) and discrediting democratic values. Defense goals entailed gaining access to secret military and economic information and assembling a network of informants.

More than 10 states, including the U.S., Great Britain, France, Germany, Spain, and Ukraine accused Moscow of trying to influence their' domestic policies, in part with the use of the newest information technologies, as evidenced by Alliance for Securing Democracy's research.[196]

In November 2016, Bulgaria elected the pro-Russian candidate Rumen Radev as president. His main opponent from the right centrist GERB party Tsetska Tsacheva accused Radev of ties with Russia. Later, five current and former Bulgarian officials told[197] *The Wall Street Journal* that Russia sent to the Bulgarian Socialist Party a 30-page "secret strategic document" with recommendations that could help Rumen Radev win the election during the presidential election campaign of 2016. Former Bulgarian President Rosen Plevneliev said that Moscow funds various political parties in Bulgaria.[198]

Almost the same thing occurred during the French

---

196 https://rus.delfi.lv/news/daily/abroad/kommersant-kakie-strany-za-poslednij-god-zayavlyali-o-vmeshatelstve-ruki-moskvy.d?id=49467061&all=true [in Russian].

197 https://www.rbc.ru/politics/23/03/2017/58d433469a79477c186229d5 [in Russian].

198 https://govoritmoskva.ru/news/113577/ [in Russian].

elections. The Kremlin's interference with presidential elections in France was first mentioned in midFebruary 2017. Emmanuel Macron's election campaign headquarters staffers said Russia used hackers and fake news in order to try to defeat Macron, who was running against the pro-Russian candidate Marine Le Pen. When Macron and Le Pen made it to the second round of elections, there was renewed talk of possible Russian interference, mentioning "Russian hackers." Right after the first round of elections, Russian hackers' interference was confirmed by the Japanese cybersecurity company *Trend Micro*, which said that hackers infected Macron's campaign headquarters computers with software that looked for vulnerabilities in the system and engaged in phishing by creating websites with names that looked like they officially represented Macron in order to trick Macron's supporters into divulging their personal data. Russia's possible influence over the French election outcome was not limited to hacking. Macron's election campaign headquarters said that Russian media spread rumors about Macron using [French] branches of *Sputnik* and RT, as well as social media, which was more actively used than TV.

Certainly Russia's attempts to affect political processes in the U.S., especially during the 2016 presidential campaign when Donald Trump ran against Hillary Clinton, attracted the most attention.

Prior to the Democratic National convention where Hillary Clinton was nominated to run for U.S. president, WikiLeaks published correspondence obtained by hacking the Democrats' e-mail. The correspondence covered the period from January 2015 to May 25, 2016 and disclosed the Democratic Party's strategy for the upcoming presidential elections.[199]

Hillary Clinton's election campaign headquarters chief John Podesta told journalists on a flight from Miami to New York that Russia was behind publishing his private correspondence on Wikileaks in order to support Clinton's opponent, the Republican Party candidate Donald Trump.

Later, in December 2016, FBI and NSA published a joint report on hacker attacks from Russia. The U.S. officially accused Russia of interfering with the 2016 elections, expelled 35 Russian diplomats, and shut down two ambassadorial residential complexes.

Two years later, on July 13, 2018,a federal grand jury charged 12 Russian intelligence officers with hacking Hillary Clinton's computer networks. An investigation determined that the defendants worked at two Russian Military Intelligence departments. An investigative group headed by special prosecutor Robert Mueller later concluded that those two departments actively conducted cyber-operations intended to interfere with the 2016 U.S. presidential elections.[200]

It didn't end with hacking and publishing the Democrats' correspondence and embarrassing Hillary Clin-

---

199 https://www.currenttime.tv/a/27876364.html [in Russian].

200 https://www.newsru.com/russia/17jul2018/gru.html [in Russian].

ton. Fake accounts appeared on Facebook and Twitter in order to spread negative, often false news in order to incite voter outrage.[201]

For example, a Facebook group called "Heart of Texas" unexpectedly called for Texans to join in a protest on May 21, 2016 against the Islamic center in Houston that had been operating there for 14 years. "Let's stop the Islamization of Texas," – group members said, publishing a photo of the Islamic Center on FB and calling it a "den of hatred." The group suggested the protesters be ready to fight: "You can bring firearms, both concealed and open!"

The "Heart of Texas" group gathered over 250,000 Facebook subscribers and was one of 470 Facebook pages believed to have been created at the Internet Research Center in St. Petersburg, Russia.

A page called "Woke Blacks" criticized Clinton for her alleged animosity toward African Americans, while another page, "United Muslims of America," showed her with a woman wearing a headscarf and said, "Support Clinton, save American Muslims!" in order to provoke a negative response.[202]

Later, it was determined that the center of the election interference operations was the Internet Research

---

201 https://www.washingtonpost.com/news/monkey-cage/wp/2018/01/05/russia-has-been-meddling-in-foreign-elections-for-decades-has-it-made-a-difference/?utm_term=.0a7888b2afaa.

202 https://www.nytimes.com/interactive/2018/09/20/us/politics/russia-interference-election-trump-clinton.html.

Agency linked to Yevgeny Prigozhin. According to investigation data, starting in 2014, the Agency started creating fake accounts on social media using names of fictitious and real people living in the U.S. These "people" pretend to be American activists and provoke discussion of painful issues: racial problems, gun ownership, inequality – everything that splits U.S. society. According to the indictment document, the goal was to "splinter the US political system."

At first, the "Agency" spread fabricated information tarnishing various candidates, but as presidential elections neared and Donald Trump was confirmed as the Republican Party presidential candidate, the Agency changed its tactic. Pretending to be members of right-wing conservative groups, "Agency" staff tried to organize pro-Trump rallies.

Russian employees spent tens of thousands of dollars on political advertising on the web. According to the charges, the operations were extensive. During its peak activity, the Internet Research Agency's monthly budget was $1.25 million.[203]

On December 17, 2018, two reports were presented to the U.S. Senate that contained the most comprehensive analysis of Prigozhin's "troll factory" activity on Facebook, Google, Instagram, and Twitter. One report was prepared by Oxford University, the other one – by researchers from New Knowledge and Columbia University. An analysis of millions of posts disseminated

203 https://www.svoboda.org/a/usa-russia-indictment/29044968.html [in Russian].

by the Internet Research Agency revealed that many accounts were paid for in rubles, contact information included Russian phone numbers, Internet Research Agency's IP addresses were seen, and activity fell sharply during New Year's holidays celebrated in Russia (December 31 and January 1).

The scope of the reach and influence was significant: the 20 most popular fake pages gathered 39 million "likes," 31 million reposts and 3.4 million comments. The audience of fake pages created by the Internet Research Agency reached 126 million Facebook users and 20 million Instagram users.

To be fair, Hillary Clinton lost the election for a number of reasons, and it is doubtful that Russian interference played a significant role.

Montenegro officials and politicians told *Time* magazine that in 2016 Oleg Deripaska and "another Russian oligarch" funded pro-Russian opposition in Montenegro before the parliamentary elections.[204] Montenegro's special prosecutor Milivoje Katnić said Russian state agencies were involved in attempting to overthrow the acting Montenegro prime minister, and the coup was planned for October 16, 2016 – the day of Skupstina elections (Skupstina is the Montenegro Parliament).[205]

---

204 http://time.com/5490169/paul-manafort-victor-boyarkin-debts/.

205 https://edition.cnn.com/2017/02/21/europe/montenegro-attempted-coup-accusation/index.html.

Mafia state methods: informal contacts

In March 2019, the German soccer club Schalke 04 played against the Manchester City team in a Champions League eighth final rematch, losing to Manchester 0:7. The Etihad stadium's VIP section included several highly-placed people and a delegation from Russia. Actually, the score is not the most important thing at such events. Much more important are the informal contacts. A year after this game, it was learned that Schalke sponsor Gazprom will supply gas to public buildings in the Manchester suburb of Salford.[206] Of course, this may have been pure coincidence.

Similar to the role of Roman Abramovich, who back in the day bought the *Chelsea* soccer club, Gazprom became an integral part of top European soccer. Fans got used to the short Gazprom video ads before each Champions League game. Gazprom did this not just to gain public support for its controversial *Severnyi Potok*-2 (Nord [Northern] Stream-2) project: the status of sponsor gave Gazprom further important advantages. The sports economist Simon Chadwick said: "Sponsorship is a kind of shell; inside the shell is a complicated network of contacts. It's the express version of quasi-diplomacy.[207] If regular channels were followed, you'd have

---

206 https://www.deutschlandfunk.de/sponsor-von-schalke-und-champions-league-wie-gazprom-den.1346.de.html?dram:article_id=496955 [in German].

207 https://www.deutschlandfunk.de/sponsor-von-schalke-und-champions-league-wie-gazprom-den.1346.de.html?dram:article_id=496955 [in German].

to stick to diplomatic protocol and wait weeks, months or even years to start talking. But when you sponsor the Champions League, you just send a few tickets to a game and say: ‘Hey, come to the game.’ Of course, he’ll say yes,” – Chadwick explained. “Sponsoring soccer helps open doors and build new networks of contacts, like an octopus whose tentacles spread from the stadium’s boxes in every direction, going everywhere.”[208]

Until February 2022, the Schalke 04 soccer club played a particularly important role in this process. Gazprom became the club’s main sponsor in 2007, at the height of discussions around building the first stage of the *Severnyi Potok* gas pipeline, which had already met with significant pushback in Europe.

It’s no wonder that Gazprom extended its sponsoring contract with Schalke 04 despite Schalke’s being relegated to Bundesliga 2. A club with a lot of debt cannot do much without sponsorship money. Rather than focusing merely on image and PR, the project became more political and diplomatic, as could be seen when the German Matthias Warnig replaced Sergei Kupriyanov (who had been responsible for Gazprom head Aleksei Miller’s PR) as the Gazprom member on Schalke’s supervisory board in 2019. Warnig was not merely a good friend of Vladimir Putin’s who proved himself numerous times on various issues and projects in Russia; Warnig was also managing director of *Nord Stream 2*.

---

208 https://www.deutschlandfunk.de/sponsor-von-schalke-und-champions-league-wie-gazprom-den.1346.de.html?dram:article_id=496955 [in German].

Only after the war with Ukraine started did Schalke end its partnership with Gazprom.

Another key that opened many European doors is the UEFA Champions League. In April 2021, a Russian joined UEFA's executive committee: Gazprom subsidiary *Gazprom Neft*'s head Aleksandr Dyukov, providing another opportunity for more intimate talks with many influential functionaries, but it all ended after the start of Russia's full-scale invasion of Ukraine.

Mafia state methods: a no-rules game

The mafia and intelligence services both work outside the law. A mafia state represents the fusion of the two, and acting outside the law or playing against the rules becomes a principle implemented in both domestic and foreign policy, and this applies to the players themselves, too.

In contrast to a regular state, the mafia state does not hold a monopoly on the right to violence; this right is franchised, so to speak. Article 359 of the Russian Criminal Code is "Mercenarism," and Recruitment, training, financing or other material provision of a mercenary, and also the use of him in an armed conflict or hostilities shall be punished by deprivation of liberty for a term of twelve to eighteen years. Participation by a mercenary in an armed conflict or hostilities shall be punished by deprivation of liberty for the term from seven up to fifteen years For a long time, using private security companies, primarily, the most well-known Wagner Group, was concealed under the official euphemism "private security activity."

The Wagner Group took part in fighting in Syria and eastern Ukraine, worked in various African regions, such as Sudan and the Central African Republic, but it was as if it did not exist. Russian journalists Orkhan Jemal, Aleksandr Rastorguyev and Kirill Radchenko, who traveled to the Central African Republic to make a film about Russian mercenaries, were murdered there. According to the Dossier Center's investigation, the Wagner Group was involved in their deaths. Private security companies are illegal, but their fighters train on official shooting ranges [delete hyphen]. The Wagner Group's main base was Krasnodar Krai's Molkino Village, not far from the deployment of the Ministry of Defense Main Intelligence Administration *Spetznaz* 10th independent brigade.[209]

After the February 2022 full-scale invasion of Ukraine, everything changed, and Wagner Group and its head Yevgeny Prigozhin received emergency powers, becoming a full-fledged private army with not just infantry but also artillery and even its own aviation. Prigozhin started personally traveling to prisons recruiting inmates to take part in fighting in Ukraine in exchange for being released from prison, although the law has no such provision and no such opportunities for prisoners. Wagner Group members recruited regular citizens, too, all over the country by promising 240,000 rubles a month.

---

209 https://www.rbc.ru/magazine/2016/09/57bac4309a79476d978e850d [in Russian].

By Putin's secret decree, Prigozhin was awarded the "Hero of Russia" star. Typical of the Wagner Group was the videotaped murder using a sledgehammer of its former mercenary and prisoner of war Yevgeny Nuzhin, and the video circulated on the web. RF law enforcement ignored that incident. Former Wagner fighter Andrei Medvedev, who fled in early January, said he knew of 10 other executions at Wagner committed in retaliation for refusing to fight in Ukraine. Medvedev said he personally witnessed several people shot to death. The Wagner Group was legalized in May 2023: when Prigozhin announced that he had taken over the Ukrainian town of Bakhmut, the Kremlin website published an official notice that the president congratulated "Wagner storm troops."[210]

The Wagner Group was created outside the law, existed outside the law, and met its sudden end outside the law. When Wagner founders Yevgeny Prigozhin and Dmitry Utkin were killed in a plane crash, few in Russia or abroad were surprised. The plane crash occurred in the most classic of *mafiosi* traditions. While accounts abounded, most people agreed that Putin did not forgive Prigozhin's June mutiny.

Expert Aleksandr Baunov noted: "If, following most Russian regime opponents and supporters, you put aside the tragic-fatalistic theory that forces of fate implement people's intentions, then Prigozhin's and the Wagner leadership's deaths show with the utmost clarity the

---

210 http://kremlin.ru/events/president/news/71172 [in Russian].

features of a mafia state, a state-grouping, characteristic of the Russian regime. It's as if the snow covering has melted, revealing the structure of the harsh northern earth."[211] Baunov noted that Prigozhin's video address from Africa released just a few hours before the plane crash indicated that a new position had been found for Prigozhin in Africa; sort of a patriotic exile with a demotion. The article rightfully notes: "However, an important punishment technique both inside a dictatorship and inside a criminal-type group is creating the false impression of peace, forgiveness, and sometimes even greater closeness to the mob boss, before destroying the enemy. As in movies about the mafia, when feuding groups and their bosses get together only to have one group shoot the other group from a cake,[212] or as in *The Godfather*, they make peace before destroying."

Incidentally, a mafia state has greater resources than the regular mafia. The mafia state sometimes even uses official armed forces outside the law, or, rather, in violation of all written and unwritten laws. That is what happened when Crimea was annexed in 2014. In late February – early March, strategic sites in Crimea were occupied by "little green men" – anonymous camouflaged people with no insignia. They were also called "polite people." In this context, a referendum was held in Crimea on unification with Russia. In a live broad-

---

211 https://carnegieendowment.org/politika/90430?fbclid=IwAR0AqYqqxyIFHQ9dtDDPphYOz4qamhD4WsG18pK16FOOqZ2rQRAAL_SoFMQ [in Russian].

212 A reference to the movie *Some Like it Hot.*

cast in April of the same year, Vladimir Putin confirmed that those green men were from the Russian Army,[213] although by law they were not supposed to be there.

Russian intelligence brazenly conducts secret illegal operations in other countries. Sometimes the secret comes to light, especially if the mission does not go as planned. For example, former Russian Military Intelligence worker Sergei Skripal and his daughter Yulia were urgently hospitalized in March 2018 in Salisbury, UK. Traces of poison (believed to be *Novichok*) used on them were found on the door handle to their house. The British authorities conducted an investigation and named the main suspects: Russians Aleksandr Petrov and Ruslan Boshirov. A while later, *Bellingcat* and *The Insider* published an investigation that proved that "Ruslan Boshirov" is actually Russian Military Intelligence Colonel and Hero of Russia Anatoly Chepiga,[214] and "Aleksandr Petrov" is Russian Military Intelligence doctor Aleksandr Mishkin.[215] In an interview to Margarita Simonyan, the two said they had traveled to Salisbury to enjoy the beauty of a local cathedral's steeple.

Petrov's and Boshirov's adventures in Salisbury are not unique. In another case, Bulgaria charged three Russians with poisoning Bulgarian businessman Emilian Gebrev, his son, and Gebrev's company director. The Bulgarian prosecutor's office said the poisoning

---

213 https://ria.ru/20140516/1007988002.html [in Russian].

214 https://theins.ru/politika/118927 [in Russian].

215 https://theins.ru/politika/121142 [in Russian].

occurred in spring 2015 using an "unidentified organophosphorus substance."[216] Emilian Gebrev's company engaged in arms sales; Gebrev himself admitted to shipping weapons to Georgia during the fighting in 2008. The Bulgarian prosecutor's office announced that individuals involved in Gebrev's poisoning were Sergei Viktorovich Pavlov, Sergei Vyacheslavovich Fedotov, and Georgi Gorshkov. The same names had appeared previously in *The Insider* and *Bellingcat*, which asserted that these individuals might be working for Russia Military Intelligence and likely traveled to Bulgaria using fictitious names and counterfeit documents.[217]

Another notorious case is the summer 2019 killing that took place in Germany, in central Berlin's *Kleiner Tiergarten* (Small Zoo) park, when Georgian citizen Zelimkhan Khangoshvili was shot to death on his way to the mosque. A Russian citizen was detained on suspicion of his murder. The German General Prosecutor's Office and the German government believe this was a hit commissioned by either Russian or Chechen authorities. In a joint investigation, *The Insider*, *Bellingcat* and *Der Spiegel* concluded that the murder suspect may have worked for Russian intelligence. On his [German] visa application, the man indicated his name is Vadim Andreevich Sokolov, 49 years old, from Irkutsk, registered as residing in St. Petersburg.

---

216 https://www.dw.com/ru/болгария-обвинила-трех-россиян-в-отравлении-бизнесмена/a-52131807 [in Russian].

217 https://www.bbc.com/russian/news-51590010 [in Russian].

Mafia state methods: collaborating with terrorist regimes

In February 2021, there was a coup in Myanmar. Members of the military arrested Myanmar President Win Myint and leader of the ruling party National League for Democracy, government advisor and head of the Ministry of Foreign Affairs Aung San Suu Kyi. The military behind the coup appointed Vice President Myint Swe as acting president while transferring all government power to chief Myanmar Armed Forces commander Min Aung Hlaing. A state of emergency was declared in Myanmar for one year, and many nations expressed concern with regard to the coup. Austria, Canada, France, Germany, Japan, New Zealand, Spain, Sweden, Turkey, Great Britain, and the U.S. condemned the coup and called for release of the detained officials. Russia did not condemn the coup. Literally a couple of weeks before the events in Myanmar, Sergei Shoigu officially visited Myanmar and discussed military and technical cooperation with the local military. In June, head of the Myanmar military *junta*, senior general Min Aung Hlaing flew to the RF to take part in a conference on international security, gave an interview to the *RIA Novosti* state agency,[218] and met with Russian Security Council Secretary Nikolai Patrushev in Moscow. Myanmar and Russian military authorities agreed on military cooperation, although the UN General Assembly

---

218 https://ria.ru/20210628/myanma-1738863740.html [in Russian].

called for suspending arms shipments to Myanmar and releasing political prisoners, with 119 countries voting in favor of the resolution; 36 countries, including Russia, China, and India, abstained. Belarus voted against the resolution. In September 2022, Min Aung Hlaing was one of the main participants in an economic forum in Vladivostok and spoke in a plenary session together with Putin. This showed that Russia is not isolated. Myanmar started buying weapons from Russia.

After the Taliban movement seized power in Afghanistan, Russia did not evacuate its embassy – on the contrary, Russia started cooperating with the new regime. Although the Taliban is a forbidden terrorist group in Russia, members of the movement are received at the highest levels in Moscow and considered "competent interlocutors." A Taliban delegation took part in the St. Petersburg Economic Forum in 2022. Whoever is not part of the democratic world, who violates human rights, becomes Russia's friend, allowing Russia to form an alternative center.

Mafia state methods: propaganda as a hybrid war method

Hybrid conflicts are conducted mainly in secret, without officially declaring war, using various intermediaries or by secret special operations in order to avoid international liability. Technological progress and digital media platforms enable significant expansion of the use of "soft power" using primarily the media.

The *Russia Today* TV channel became the main tool of Russian media and political influence abroad. The channel started operating in 2005. Former special correspondent of the *Rossiya* channel in the Kremlin pool, 25year old Margarita Simonyan was appointed head of the RT channel.

RT welcomed commentators and "experts" who had little chance of appearing on any other media platform in the West: anarchists, anti-globalists, members of various radical right-wing and radical left-wing movements. After rebranding, the channel's name became RT. Starting in April 2012, RT broadcast a series organized by Wikileaks founder Julian Assange. Episode 1 of the series included an interview with Hezbollah leader Hassan Nasrallah. RT gains its audience's trust with neutral and sometimes even entertaining content, but when reporting on events and figures important to Russia, it always takes unambiguous positions.

Staci Bivens is a former RT correspondent in the U.S. In March 2014, she told BuzzFeed "how the truth is made" on the TV channel. Several years earlier, RT leadership asked her to do a story saying that Germany is a failed state. "They called me in and it was really surreal. One of the managers said, 'The story is that the West is failing, Germany is a failed state,'" Bivens said in disbelief. She tried arguing, tried to prove this wasn't true; that the term "failed state" is reserved for countries such as Somalia or Congo, not for economically advanced, industrialized nations such as Germany. Bivens refused to do what the management wanted. Nevertheless, the channel sent a film crew to Germany without her.

Bivens did not immediately resign, but her contract was ending soon, and she decided not to renew it.[219]

Mafia state methods: wars of aggression

On February 24, 2022 Vladimir Putin addressed Russian citizens, announcing the start of a "special military operation" in Ukraine, saying: "Its goal is to protect people who, for eight years, have been subjected to humiliation and genocide from the Kyiv regime. To do that, we will strive to demilitarize and de-nazify Ukraine, and prosecute those who committed numerous bloody crimes against civilians, including Russian Federation citizens." The president noted that NATO expansion is unacceptable, and all actions represent self-defense from the created threats. This was preceded by a February 21 [Russian] Security Council session, televised almost in its entirety, with every participant speaking on-camera in support of recognizing the independence of the People's Republics of Donetsk and Luhansk.[220] This looked like an attempt to make everyone complicit, in the best mafia tradition. Russia acknowledged the People's Republics of Donetsk and Luhansk, and signed agreements with them on friendship, cooperation, and mutual aid.

---

219 https://www.buzzfeednews.com/article/rosiegray/how-the-truth-is-made-at-russia-today.

220 The so-called DPR and LPR are separatist territorial entities that existed 2014 – 2022 as self-proclaimed nations and were then annexed by Russia.

For weeks, Russia amassed troops at the Ukrainian border, explaining both to the world and to its own military that these are merely exercises. But then the Russian forces crossed the border, starting a real war, although Russia prohibited use of the word "war"; permissible words are "special operation" or "special military operation."

What did Russia receive as a result? Unprecedented sanctions that threaten to destroy the Russian economy. Nothing similar had ever happened before in the world. Over 6,650 types of various sanction were imposed on Russia, and, counting the sanctions already in place prior to February 22, they total over 8,000. Major Western companies ceased their operations in Russia, and shipments of all kinds of goods stopped. Europe, the main consumer of Russian hydrocarbons, decided to stop its gas dependency on Russia, which had been most likely Russia's main tool of influence.

Russia was expelled from numerous international organizations, including the Council of Europe. The UN General Assembly voted to suspend Russia's membership in the Human Rights Council, with 93 nations voting "for," 24 voting "against," and 58 abstaining. Belarus, Iran, China, Kyrgyzstan, Kazakhstan, Tajikistan, Uzbekistan, Syria, Vietnam, Zimbabwe, Laos, Mali, Nicaragua, Eritrea, Ethiopia, Cuba, Congo DR, Burundi, Bolivia, Democratic People's Republic of Korea, and Gabon supported Russia. These countries are Russia's main allies in the international arena. This was the second case in history: in 2011, Libya was expelled from the UN Human Rights Council after Moammar Gaddafi's regime violently suppressed protests, but Libya's membership was restored eight months later, after Gaddafi was overthrown.

Another result backfired against Russia: Finland and Sweden expressed the desire to join NATO, meaning NATO will be even closer, as the Finnish border is just 150 km. (93 miles) from St. Petersburg, Russia.

Millions of refugees fled Ukraine, including many people whose mother tongue is Russian. Thousands of civilians, including children, were killed in Ukraine. According to official UN data, between the start of Russia's full-scale invasion of Ukraine and the end of June 2023, the dead and wounded numbered 25,170 civilians,[221] with the actual number of those killed probably much higher. On March 17, 2023, the Russian government's criminal nature was affirmed at the international level, when the International Criminal Court in the Hague issued an arrest warrant for RF President Vladimir Putin and the Presidential Commissioner for Children's Rights Maria Lvova-Belova, charging them with war crimes for illegally deporting children from Ukraine to Russia.

The mafia state's ideology

In a mafia state, ideology is a tool used to keep the ruling

221 https://ukraine.un.org/sites/default/files/2023-07/Civilian%20casualties%20in%20Ukraine%20from%2024%20Feb%202022%20to%2030%20June%202023%20ENG.pdf.

group in power. This is an important difference between the mafia state and totalitarian regimes, where ideology is the basis for state building. At various times, mafia state authorities use whatever narratives they need in order to meet their current objectives.

Early Putin: the idea of "stability"

Putin's ideology in the early phase was formed around the idea of "stability" counterposed to "the chaos of the 1990s," the Yeltsin era and market reforms, which became a convenient bugaboo. The question: "So you want it to be like it was in the 1990s?" was typical of the regime's rhetoric. The assumption was that no one wants to trade the Putin era's stability for renewed "chaos and lawlessness" reminiscent of Yeltsin's era.

Gradually, the idea of stability was transformed into the concept of the permanence of power. It was affirmed that only keeping Vladimir Putin as leader of the nation could guarantee citizens stability and the quality of life that had been achieved to a large degree due to the oil and gas market. This idea reached its peak when Russia's very existence was equated to Vladimir Putin's being in power. In 2014, RF Presidential Administration First Deputy Head Vyacheslav Volodin said: "If there is Putin, there is Russia, and if there is no Putin, there is no Russia."

Reliance on the "great past," nostalgia for the USSR

Relying on "the great past," the Russian mafia state tries not only to prove its legitimacy but also to assert its special rights, including the right to engage in foreign aggression.

The regime members' propaganda and rhetoric use nostalgia for the empire, and build a myth of Great Russia as successor to the USSR, a powerful, dominant country that was respected and feared all over the world. A sense of pride in the nation and its power becomes a mainstay of propaganda, easily topping, for much of the Russian population, such values as human rights and a good, quiet life. Exploiting images of the past helps those in power easily to collect political dividends. Restoring the empire becomes the image of Russia's future. Today's strength is drawn from yesterday.

In December 2022, 63% of Russians polled were nostalgic for the USSR, according to the Public Opinion Foundation, which is 12% higher than in 2011, but lower than in 2001, when Vladimir Putin first came to power: in 2001, 76% of those polled "regretted" that the USSR had ceased to exist, with the record 85% feeling that way in late 1999, after the default that crushed the hopes of stable economic development and fast positive results. Naturally, the regime invariably began exploiting this nostalgia in its propaganda.

Starting in the early 2000s, TV broadcasts that have long been serving the mafia state's interests successfully created the impression among viewers that Soviet times are continuing. To this end, Soviet movies and shows are re-broadcast non-stop along with old Soviet songs performed by the same singers. The illusion of "returning to the USSR" is used in sports, too, with hockey players dressed in uniforms worn by victorious Soviet teams. The uniform doesn't help them win, of course, but it does arouse revanchist moods.

"Soviet" and "Russian" gradually intermix and begin to be perceived as one and the same. The Soviet Union germinates in modern Russia, making it not just its successor, but almost as if it were the Soviet Union itself.

The Russian mafia state misappropriates the USSR's legacy, highlighting the "great pages of history and victories" but obliterating the memory of the Soviet regime's crimes and responsibility for those crimes. The red flag and the USSR national anthem are reinstated, WWII history is presented exclusively as the history of the Soviet soldier's victorious march in Europe and the liberation of Europe. The state always talks of itself as the victor, but never as a criminal.

In April 2022, after the Russian army took control of the Ukrainian town of Henichesk, Lenin's statue was symbolically restored as the first order of business, and flags of the RF and USSR were raised above city hall. In January 2023, authorities of the town of Melitopol, which was now under Russian control, renamed 86 city streets and sites, restoring their old Soviet names. For example, Vishnevaya and Yaltinskaya Streets became streets named after the 40th anniversary and the 60th anniversary of the October Revolution, commemorating the Bolshevik Revolution of 1917. Melitopol once again saw streets named after Lenin, Voikov, Frunze, and other Soviet military and Communist Party figures along with street names such as Kommunarov, Komsomolskaya, Proletarskaya, Pionerskaya, and others. In part, this was done in reaction to the decommunization process in Ukraine and "Lenin toppling" – when starting in 2013-2014, monuments that symbolized the Soviet past and connection with it were being dismantled all over Ukraine. Very probably, those events were too painful for the Russian regime and signaled symbolically that Ukraine was no longer under Russia's imperial influence.

The figure of Joseph Stalin became an important element in the idea of a return to the USSR, and statues of Stalin started appearing in several cities. There were numerous discussions about renaming the city of Volgograd [back] to Stalingrad. The authorities, however, have not yet decided to go all the way, finding a middle ground. For example, the name "Heroic City of Stalingrad" became the symbol for Volgograd, and is used interchangeably with the name Volgograd. In 2022, during celebrations of the victory in the Battle of Stalingrad, new "Stalingrad" road signs were installed at the entrance to Volgograd.

EMPIRE AS AN IDEAL

The ideal form of Putin's modern Russia is proclaimed to be a powerful empire. Citizens and propagandists dream of it, trying to prove its inevitability and inscribing it into historic continuity: "There were five Russian empires in Russian history. The first Empire was Kyiv-Novgorod, personified by the saintly Prince Vladimir. The second empire was the Tsardom of Muscovy with its founder, Tsar Ivan Vasilievich Grozny [Ivan the Terrible]. The third empire was the Romanov Empire with its powerful ruler Peter the Great. The fourth empire is the Red Empire of Joseph Stalin. And today's empire is the fifth empire created by Vladimir Putin."[222]

Deeming itself a Soviet or post-Soviet empire, modern Russia believes it has a historical right to interfere in post-Soviet countries' life, influencing their development and their chosen path. Russia believes it can serve as a guarantor of post-Soviet countries' sovereignty and independence, which is exactly what Putin declared in 2022 regarding Ukraine: "Only Russia can be a real, serious guarantor of Ukrainian statehood, sovereignty and territorial integrity."[223]

---

222 https://histrf.ru/images/RVIO_7_2022.pdf [in Russian].

223 https://ria.ru/20221027/putin-1827302538.html [in Russian].

The Russian mafia state is an imperial state that builds its image on grandeur and power directed not inwardly, but outwardly; it believes that its mission is to extend control over territories, subjects, and resources.

Victory as a New Religion

The modern Russian state relies on the "Great Victory" in WWII as the main foundation of its existence. The victory in that war substantiates the current regime's political course and legitimacy.

Under Putin, the USSR's WWII victory was elevated into a holy cult, a symbol of faith, and a new militant religion started forming around it. Even cathedrals were built in the name of Victory, with symbols of this new religion displayed in the cathedrals. For example, on June 22, 2020, the Victory Cathedral, also known as The Main Cathedral of the RF Armed Forces, was opened. The building itself, its architecture and decoration are overloaded with symbolism linking the ideas of Christianity, messianism, images of the holy Russian military and its victories, especially the victory in the Great Patriotic War (WWII).

The Cathedral building glorifies Great Prince Vladimir, Sainted Equal of the Apostles, in whose honor the lower cathedral is consecrated, where Prince Vladimir's 6-meter (20 ft) image is carved in bas-relief. In one of the Cathedral's inner halls, there is a mosaic of Prince Vladimir's baptism in Chersonese, emphasizing the stance that Crimea is historically Russian. The figure of Prince Vladimir, who baptized Russia and conquered Kyiv, is relentlessly paralleled to images and actions by Vladimir Putin.

Even the Armed Forces Cathedral's technical properties are explained not using architectural or construction norms, but by the symbolism of a Religion of Victory":

75 years ago	**75** meters – height of the bell tower
May **8, 1945**	**19.45** meters – diameter of the dome drum, which has **8** windows
at **22:43**, Germany's Instrument of Unconditional Surrender was signed	**22.43** meters – dome diameter
End of the war that lasted **1,418** days and nights	**14.18** meters – small dome height
960 –Great Prince Saint Vladimir, Equal of the Apostles was born	**96** meters – height counting the lower cathedral

The Cathedral's memorial complex holds Hitler's suit and cap. Church porticos are made from war trophy arms. The Cathedral is painted a khaki color, its tall dome-topped towers are reminiscent of ballistic missiles pointed to the sky. Inside are memorial stones with brass cartridges filled with dirt taken from graves of Soviet soldiers killed in WWII and buried in Armenia, Belgium, Latvia, Turkmenistan, the Czech Republic, and Switzerland.

Victory in WWII is the main cult object of the "Religion of Victory." Another event that this religion imbues with symbolic, religious meaning is another victory, "the homecoming of Crimea to Russia." Initially, plans called for installing a mosaic representing the reunification of Crimea with Russia in 2014 inside the Victory Cathedral. The mosaic featured Putin, Sergei Shoigu, Security Council secretary Nikolai Patrushev, FSB director Aleksandr Bortnikov, State Duma speaker Vyacheslav Volodin, armed forces chief of general staff Valery Gerasimov, Minister of Foreign Affairs Sergei Lavrov, former Putin bodyguard Aleksei Dyumin, and Federation Council head Valentina Matvienko. The same panel shows gleeful people holding the banner "Crimea is Ours," as well as "polite people" – the soldiers from Russian special units who gained control over Crimea in 2014. The idea behind placing this mosaic in the cathedral was to perpetuate a new iconostasis, new saints of the "Religion of Victory." After a public scandal, Putin ordered the mosaic removed, and it was placed elsewhere in temporary storage.

Starting in the 2010s, the May 9th [Russian] WWII Victory Day celebration more and more continued to change from a Memorial Day to a day of demonstrating readiness for a future war. The fewer living WWII veterans remained, the more attention shifted away from pride over their heroism, from mourning and memory over to pride over [Russia's] tanks and missiles. The Victory Parade was becoming more of a show demonstrating the might of Russian weaponry and its army, a sacral act in the "Religion of Victory."

New popular slogans were heard, such as "Thank you, grandpa, for the Victory!" "We can do it again!" and "Onward to Berlin!" and people willingly put these bumper stickers on their cars, governed by inner rectitude and an ever-growing feeling of revanchism.

The "Immortal Regiment," movement, which first arose as a civil memorial movement aiming at preserving family memories of war, was appropriated by the regime and started playing a mobilizing function – the citizens' readiness to form ranks and go to war, following their grandfathers and great-grandfathers. A "parading" of the perception of war occurred – not just WWII, but any other war, too. The war's tragic component, memories of the victims receded into the background, and what remained in the forefront were the ceremonial parade and glorification of death, with death described as joyful and welcome because it occurs in the name of a "higher purpose," "dying for the Motherland," and dying in a "holy war" washes away all past sins and purifies the person.

In the new "Religion of Victory," the Soviet (aka Russian) army acquired the status of "invincible" and was endowed with holiness and heroic infallibility. This army liberates the people of the world from enemies, acting fairly, powerfully, and precisely. It is not only a "victorious army," it is also a "liberation army." These propagandist catchphrases successfully were embedded in the fertile soil of Russian citizens' trust in the Russian army. This trust is related partially to the fact that in many Russian regions, especially the poorest ones, the army is the only accessible way to attain a higher social status. This explains why in spring 2022 many Russians simply could not believe what happened in the Ukrainian town of Bucha. People simply could not conceive that the "heroic liberation army" could commit such crimes.

An important part of the "Religion of Victory" was recreating the "grand style" – a fusion of the new religion and televised large-scale actions using the latest technology. This "grand style" intensifies the emotional aura around victory, becoming an important tool of sanctifying and glorifying it. "Grand style" is the increasingly powerful demonstration of military technology, with plane formations flying right above Red Square. It's the TV broadcast of the May 9th parades, ever more technically advanced and ever more dazzling. It is also the symbolic orchestral concerts conducted by Valery Gergiev in Tskhinvali (Ossetia) and Palmyra (Syria), held at sites of cruel executions and barbaric destruction.

Incidentally, sometimes the mafia state extends its tentacles directly into the pompous "grand style" productions. For example, taking part in the Palmyra concert was St. Petersburg House of Music director, the cellist Sergei Roldugin, who performed a solo during the performance of a quadrille. Roldugin is not merely a cellist, he is also an old and very close friend of Vladimir Putin. Roldugin gained fame not as musician, but as owner of several multi-billion dollar offshore companies that made strange deals with Russian state-owned companies, prompting several international investigations into money laundering.

Concerts in recently destroyed cities are an important element of the "Religion of Victory" and "grand style." They symbolically parallel the performance of Shostakovich's 7th Symphony in besieged Leningrad, which "the religion of war" presents as having led to victory. As in any religion, repeating symbolic gestures must lead to a repetition of the result, in this case a victory.

Another aspect of the "grand style" is the "Immortal Regiment" march, which ideologists imbue with sacral meaning, literally comparing it to the "Easter parade of Russian resurrection." TV images of the "Immortal Regiment" march lead by Vladimir Putin, with marchers holding portraits of the deceased instead of icons, truly recall the Easter processions of the late nineteenth – early twentieth century, although, instead of parading into a cathedral they end up in Red Square, at the center of power.

"Grand style" within the framework of the "Religion of Victory" is also the storming of a cardboard Reichstag and the tank biathlon that became a regular event after Sergei Shoigu became minister of defense. Another aspect of "grand style" is the rallies in support of the authorities' decisions, attendance at which counts as paid work time and is obligatory for state employees. The rallies are intended to create the needed propagandist image of people coming together in support of the regime. "Grand style" is also using human bodies, including children, to form the Russian victory symbol of the war in Ukraine – the letter Z.

Other symbols of the "grand style" are the Crimean bridge, large-scale construction projects, and the Sochi

Olympics, during which Russian athletes were tasked with winning at any cost because only that outcome fits in with the "Religion of Victory." In this religion, the main objective is instilling a victorious spirit in the population and convincing them that it must win. The collapse of the Soviet Union is presented as a defeat and catastrophe after which the Russian people forgot about their victories.

The "Religion of Victory" is closely tied also to traditional Russian Orthodoxy. Here, the God of the Christian religion serves as commander-in-chief of the Russian military. It is no accident that the website of the Main Cathedral of the Russian Armed Forces opens with an epigraph ascribed to the noted eighteenth century Russian military hero General Alexander V. Suvorov: "Pray to God; Victory comes from Him. God is our General, He is leading us."

One of the unofficial slogans of the war against Ukraine is the phrase "We are Russian, God is with us!" This means that God protects and intervenes specifically on behalf of Russians – or, more specifically, the Russian army, which belief, incidentally, goes back to the early nineteenth century, when the war of 1812 was interpreted ideologically, and the mystical link between God, Victory and Russia was born.

One of the "Religion of Victory" ideologists Aleksandr Prokhanov insists that the "mystical victory of 1945" has "divine meaning" and "atones for all the persecutions and beatings, the monstrous injustice and violence with Christ-like sacrifice by the Soviet people, who placed almost 30 million of their sons and daughters on the altar of Victory." Prokhanov writes that "victory is precious to us not just for its past, but also for its future... Victory represents the precious common cause for which our people yearn."

In the "Religion of Victory," sacrifice and death during war are holy and necessary; they lead the deceased to "God's Kingdom." Vladimir Putin formulated this thesis himself, ascribing a sacred meaning to death in a nuclear war: "We, as martyrs, shall go to Heaven, but they [the enemies] will just croak." In the "Religion of Victory," "divine providence" is said to lead the people through cruel suffering (purifying) that will lead to victory.

Messianism and imperialism are inherent in the "Religion of Victory," which promotes the notion that the Russian people must liberate neighboring peoples, bring peace to their lands, end suffering, save them from enemies or troubles. Within the framework of the "Religion of Victory," Russian military campaigns are always liberating and messianic; they always have a higher purpose and mission that goes beyond victory over the enemy.

Anti-liberalism and Traditional Values

At the beginning of the twenty-first century, the Russian mafia state leadership declared that liberalism is not merely harmful but also a true enemy. Liberalism (together with the "collective West" as its proponent) was presented as responsible for the collapse of the USSR and the reason for the potential ruin of Russia. The regime contends that only *de facto* rejecting the liberal idea made it possible to save the country at the start of this century. Western liberalism is termed the main world view opponent of Russia, and many propagandists are incensed that its ideas are still enshrined in Article I of the RF Constitution, which "constantly nurtures and breeds national traitors, the fifth column."

The mafia state's rhetoric is built on anti-liberalism and the constant appeal to "traditional values," which, however, are almost never spelled out. In their public rhetoric, Vladimir Putin, Nikolai Patrushev, and Dmitry Medvedev try to convince everyone that liberal ideas subvert "traditional Russian values." In order to preserve traditional Russian values, they are even enshrined in the 2020 Constitutional amendments. "The West's war against Russia" supposedly is fought with the aim of destroying traditional Russian values and implanting harmful values through "eroding the traditions of various peoples that formed over centuries, including their language, faith and the historical memory of generations." Putin and Patrushev especially focus on the danger of "implanting LGBT values," which they believe lead to destroying families and to "Russia's dying out." They reject the values of human rights, freedom of speech, freedom of conscience, economic and political rights.

In one of his articles, Nikolai Patrushev formulates Russia's alternative proposal: "Unlike the West, Russia, in essence, offers a new civilizational choice that includes equality, justice, non-interference in domestic affairs, the absence of a patronizing tone or any preliminary conditions for mutually advantageous cooperation. Russia proposes granting national sovereignty (including cultural sovereignty and spiritual and moral sovereignty) the status of the greatest value and the basis of the subsequent building of human civilization."[224] Notably, in this concept, Russia's sovereignty extends to the entire post-Soviet territory, especially Slavic countries, which, in this concept, are "historically Russian territories."

A special role in maintaining traditional values is played by Eastern Orthodoxy and the Russian Orthodox Church; they are called upon to engage in the "moral upbringing" of society and support the society's "spiritual values."

---

224 https://rg.ru/2020/06/17/nuzhny-li-rossii-universalnye-cennosti.html?ysclid=lm4pqsk69i645707464 [in Russian].

Anti-Westernism and anti-liberalism go hand in hand in a mafia state's ideology. Any ties with the West – cultural, scientific, technological, and of course financial – are denounced as harmful to the stability and life of the mafia state.

The idea of sovereignty

The idea of sovereignty is supreme for Putin's ideology as a whole. Sovereignty means that a state pursues an independent policy, based on its own history, its traditional values. At least in words. In practice, however, the idea of sovereignty becomes the idea of a rogue state, a state that is a besieged fortress that does not take part in international institutions, and is closed off from any influence – cultural, media, or economic, as such influence is deemed harmful. Such a state becomes solitary, stripped of support and understanding. What's more, what often hides behind the word "sovereignty" is merely the ruler's desire to do what he wants. In connection with such an interpretation of the idea of sovereignty, a mafia state develops the concept according to which countries can be divided into those that have true sovereignty and those that do not. Countries without sovereignty inevitably end up with a feudal status and become dependent on countries that do have sovereignty.

According to Vladimir Putin's exposition, one of the main world processes now is the U.S. and the West's attempting to strip other countries of sovereignty:

The West has been looking all this time and continues to look for a new chance to hit us, weaken and destroy Russia, which they have always dreamed of, split our state, pit peoples against each other, doom them to poverty and extinction. They are simply haunted by the fact that there is such a great, huge country in the world with its territory, natural wealth, resources, with a people who do not know how and will never live according to someone else's orders.

The West is ready to step over everything in order to preserve the neo-colonial system that allows it to parasitize, in fact, to plunder the world at the expense of the power of the dollar and technological dictates, to collect real tribute from humanity, to extract the main source of unearned prosperity, the rent of the hegemon. The maintenance of this rent is their key, genuine and absolutely self-serving motive. That is why total desovereignization is in their interests. Hence their aggression towards independent states, towards traditional values and original cultures, attempts to undermine international and integration processes beyond their control, new world currencies and centers of technological development. It is critical for them that all countries surrender their sovereignty to the United States.[225]

---

225 https://www.miragenews.com/full-text-of-putins-speech-at-annexation-866383/.

A new ideology: justification of the war

With the start of Russia's aggression toward Ukraine, Russian authorities and propagandists started using a new ideological narrative justifying Russia's actions in the war.

The key components of this narrative are:

- Ukraine is not an independent state. "Ukraine" is a quasi-state behind which are forces of the "collective West." Russia, therefore, is fighting not Ukraine, but the "collective West" in Ukraine. This is the West's war against the Slavic people and the "Russian world."
- Russia defends its Fatherland, which the West seeks to dismantle. Russia's very existence is at stake. Losing the war will result in the destruction of Russia, and the Russian people cannot permit this.
- This is a "patriotic, holy, liberating war" around which the entire society is consolidated. All who are against the war are enemies of Russia and traitors. The Russian people are ready to fight, ready to sacrifice themselves, and on this foundation, victory will be achieved. God is with us, and the truth is on our side.

An important component of justification of the war against Ukraine is describing it as the continuation of the unfinished Great Patriotic War (WWII): "We did not take victory all the way, we did not finish the war, we did not fully purge Europe of Fascism. Ten postwar years were spent liquidating underground gangs in Western Ukraine, but the idea continued to live in the minds of some Ukrainians up to the collapse of the USSR. When the Soviet people were disillusioned with Communism, its place in Ukraine was quickly taken first by nationalism, then by its extreme form – Nazism. Its ideological victory was not accidental."[226]

Dmitry Medvedev writes about this on his *Telegram* channel: "Our country defeated Napoleon and Hitler. <...> Therefore, Ukrainian Nazis and Western Europe are direct heirs of those who fought against Russia. And war against them, thus, is a new Patriotic War, and victory will be ours, as it was in 1812 and 1945."[227]

---

226 https://histrf.ru/read/articles/denacifikaciya-germanii-i-ukrainy-obshchee-i-osobennoe [in Russian].

227 https://t.me/medvedev_telegram/253 [in Russian].

Conspiracy theories

In a mafia state, conspiracy theories become the basis for political decisions and political action.

Belief in various conspiracy theories is rather typical of modern society, as was confirmed during the coronavirus pandemic and the widespread anti-Vax movement in Russia and elsewhere. Some believed "the population was being micro-chipped," that "the virus was man-made," and so forth. Most conspiracy theories are very easy to understand and simplistic; they ignore the complexity of the world, rendering the world flat and comprehensible. Explaining occurrences by alluding to someone's evil intent and conspiracy simplifies life and reduces anxiety.

In a mafia state, the authorities start relying on conspiracy theories in decision making. There is reason to believe that Putin decided to go to war against Ukraine because he and those around him were convinced there was a conspiracy to weaken and destroy Russia. And intelligence reports were tailored to this theory.

This conspiracy theory can essentially be summarized as follows: "*Real power in the West is in the hands of transnational corporations that have resources. In aspiring to dominate the world, they took control over heads of state, turning them into their puppets. They pump out resources from other countries. They try to impose false values, such as LGBT. They tried to destroy and take control of Russia, too, in the 1990s, but they failed; therefore, they started a war against Russia using Ukraine. The purpose of this war is to weaken and dismember Russia, seize its natural resources and annihilate the Russian people."*

Vladimir Putin, Nikolai Patrushev, Sergei Lavrov, Patriarch Kirill, and many other mafia state figures construct their public speeches around that conspiracy theory. This theory is actively spread by propaganda, and the already-indoctrinated Russian public readily welcomes it, impelling the population to close ranks around the authorities and Putin and rise to defend the Motherland.

Loss of agency

A conspiracy theory presumes that no forces in the world (aside from the U.S., the West and transnational corporations) have their own agency and freedom of will, meaning they do not act independently – they follow orders, as puppets of some "puppeteers." According to this world view, there are no civil or public movements or organizations; they never exist unless someone pays for and organizes them. There are no "angry citizens" who would protest simply because they do not like something. According to promoters of such a worldview, no revolution or public unrest happens spontaneously, as a result of a cumulative effect; revolutions or unrest, supposedly, are always the result of someone's evil plan and invested resources.

In trying to justify the war in Ukraine, Russian authorities therefore pushed the concept that the Ukrainian Orange revolution of 2004 and The Revolution of Dignity in 2013-2014 were planned, organized, and paid for by the "collective West" and the U,S,, and, consequently, Ukraine was managed from the outside, losing its independence and sovereignty.

Key to Russian propaganda was the very idea of "color revolutions" as the U.S.'s main tool for restructuring the world. Russia's main goal as a state, therefore, becomes avoiding the manipulator – the U.S., returning Russia's historic agency (sovereignty), and ending the dependency imposed by the U.S. in the 1990s. The war with Ukraine thus is seen as returning agency to the Russian people: "This year became a turning point in Russian history: The Russian people returned to History as a subject and no longer an object or a tool in someone else's hands. In 2022, Russians returned to world history in order to protect themselves and make the world more just."[228] The Russian regime does not view the Ukrainian state as an independent entity, which is why Russia allows itself to use any methods of war.

---

228 https://www.osnmedia.ru/opinions/samyj-russkij-god-stoletiya-kakim-vojdyot-v-istoriyu-2022-j/ [in Russian].

Rejecting responsibility and depoliticization

A conspiracy theory is well received in traumatized societies that voluntarily give up responsibility and influence.

Magyar describes this process as follows: "A person or a nation that gives up responsibility for their fate, who counts on the state's taking care of them, needs fairy tales regarding who warped their fate and stole their happiness and why. It's a straight path from endless justification to irritated searches for a scapegoat. The scapegoats can be people 'who don't have souls like ours,' Commies, bankers, oligarchs, offshore warriors, liberals, Jews, Gays, Gypsies – in general, anyone, even if they don't exist."

Inhabitant instead of citizen

The mafia state prefers citizens to become subjects, "inhabitants" who give up some of their rights in exchange for the feeling of the country's greatness.

An inhabitant is loyal, dependent on the state, and lives at the state's expense. An inhabitant is distanced from governing the state, he should not interfere in politics, protest, or try to contest the mafia clan's power. In exchange for this loyalty, the mafia state compensates the inhabitant, enabling the inhabitant to live and provide himself with minimal food and clothing.

According to data of the Russian Federal State Statistics Service, gathered on the basis of the Russian 2021 census, 33%, or 42.7 million people, live on money from the state – pensions, unemployment assistance, and numerous social benefits. For 31 million people, these payments are the primary means of subsistence.

According to ING analysts' data, in 2021, the number of Russians dependent on payments from the state exceeded 60 million people, or 42% of the country's population. If you count only people employed at state entities (government officials, military personnel, teachers), then that number is 17.5 million people. If you add pensioners to this number, (43 million), then it's over 60 million people.

Let's add to these numbers the 12.9% of the able-bodied population that works at state corporations (according to OECD data). This means the state employs almost one out of three Russian adults. This, to a large extent, is reminiscent of the situation in the Soviet Union, where there were no independent workers; everyone worked for the state and in the state's interests. Not their own interests, but the state interests, which were announced and explained to Soviet people on TV: make more tanks, build more missiles, fulfill the five-year state plan.

In exchange for loyalty, the mafia state also guarantees that it won't interfere with the life of the ordinary inhabitant, letting him live however he wants and even work on the side, i. e., earning additional untaxed income. The state guarantees that it won't interfere with the inhabitant's private life, won't touch his body and his life. This last guarantee, however, is revoked during crisis times: during the coronavirus pandemic, the state tried to force inhabitants to get mandatory vaccines but was met with rather frenzied resistance. During the war against Ukraine, inhabitants had to be mobilized because of the failure of the initial plan of dealing with Ukraine quickly and bloodlessly, as was done with Crimea and using only professional military units.

An inhabitant has no agency; he's always the subject of manipulations and decisions by those in power. An inhabitant is mobilized, recruited to Wagner, jailed, and handled like an object. That's why an object can be killed, tortured, raped, and unfairly treated in the name of the state. The inhabitant always complains that some mysterious *"they"* promised something but didn't keep their word, didn't pay, didn't provide. An inhabitant simply waits until "they" will fulfill their promises.

The value of an inhabitant's own life is also questionable. An inhabitant's life is not valuable to either the mafia system or to himself, and all the easier to give up this life if "the Motherland says so." An inhabitant feels fully dependent on the state, and, therefore, fully indebted to it. In particular, an inhabitant obediently goes to war and obediently dies there. Inhabitants live according to orders and heed orders. Freedom of choice and freedom of decision making are a heavy burden, which the inhabitant transfer to the state. Inhabitants also leave up to the state issues regarding their own income, including pay raises, believing the state must make those decisions.

The inhabitant feels no responsibility for the mafia state authorities' decisions; he believes the authorities know better; "they don't tell us everything." An inhabitant distances himself from the authorities, he is fully alienated from them. Sociological research conducted after the February full-scale invasion of Ukraine using focus groups clearly showed that inhabitants don't feel responsible for the war in Ukraine, its civilian victims, and so forth.

One reason for the failure to form a civil society is that people lack anything they could value and defend. Many own no significant property or even their own housing. People do not create new property through their work. Less than 2% of the Russian population are entrepreneurs, and this number is plummeting because it is more advantageous to the mafia state to have people dependent on it, instead of independent subjects who, if they sense their independence, may try to change the political system or usurp power. This is why the mafia state makes it impossible to amass a large amount of capital unless the mafia controls it.

The Mafia state does not permit individuals who count on their own resources to come into their own. In Putin's circle, essentially all prominent figures in it (with rare exceptions) are appointees who received power and property not through their own efforts and merits but through closeness to the mafia clan. The mafia state therefore destroys anyone who has his own resources, whether a journalist, an artist, or a businessman. Such an individual's resources are taken away (or destroyed), and the individual is declared "a foreign agent," is jailed, forced to emigrate, or is killed. The mafia state fears people who are not inhabitants, people with freedom of choice, people not following orders. This is precisely why, in a mafia state, it is impossible to have independent politics based on citizens who are not subservient to the mafia state.

Language as an instrument of propaganda

The mafia state's language is the language of hoodlums, the street, and petty criminals. It's woven from slang, vulgarity, degrading and derogatory words. It is the language of aggression, antagonism, and hatred.

A Mafia state leader's subconscious sometimes gives rise to indecent associations that break through the language.

RF President Vladimir Putin said regarding Ukraine: "*So you don't think it's fun, I still won't stop until I'm done.*" Looking at the context of this phrase uttered by a head of state leaves one puzzled. Having the head of a *mafia* state saying it seems organic. This particular saying derived from the "low" language of dirty poems:

"A beauty in her coffin sleeps,

I sneak up, insert my d***,

So you don't think it's fun,

I still won't stop until I'm done."

Such rhetoric could be explained by the fact that Vladimir Putin spent his childhood and youth in Leningrad back alleys, but he is not the only one using such language. Here are some other examples:

"Pardon my language, but we don't give two shits about the Western sanctions," declared RF Ambassador to Sweden Viktor Tatarintsev.

RF Ministry of Foreign Affairs Sergei Lavrov said: "The dude said it, and the dude did it."

Federation Council Deputy Chairman and United Russia General Council Secretary Andrei Turchak said: "You piss on their eyes, and they think it's divine dew."

Mafia state language is a unique blend of criminal slang and Russian bureaucratic lexicon. Whereas the early USSR was marked by revolutionary newspeak, in the twenty-first century, newspeak typical of a mafia state was synthesized in Russia.

Mafia state language is based on slang and vulgarity, focusing on what's below the waist. This is typical of criminal language. Linguists note that criminal slang "overflows with anal and genital topics" (Baldaev 1992: 8). Vladimir Putin, too, is somewhat fixated on this topic. In 2006, when answering a question regarding possible sanctions against Iran, he said: "If grandma had certain sexual features, she'd be grandpa. Politics does not tolerate the conditional tense." Putin repeated this in 2014 when talking to journalists in Milan. In September 2022, Putin said something new when meeting with schoolchildren: "Hard work isn't just a rubber butt."

The mafia state language is full of metaphors, double-entendres, and omissions typical of classic mafia language. There are many restrictions on what may be said and how it is said. One blatant example is Putin's longstanding pathological avoidance of the name Navalny. Instead, Putin calls him "the Berlin patient," "the defendant," or "the passenger."

Mafia state language is proscriptive, it is prohibited to say many words in public, and things are not called by their real names. Instead of "explosion," the non-scary word "pop" is used; "retreat" becomes a "gesture of goodwill." Describing the special military operation as a "war" is a criminal offence.

Mafia state language aims at consolidation and mobilization by dividing the world into "one of us" and "enemies."

This language employs techniques designed to instruct, demonstrate, label, and stigmatize. This is not a language of discussion, it is the language of a shout, an order. The language starts forming an identity, giving rise to concepts like "one of us," "insiders" whom we "do not abandon" and whom "we protect." If you are not "one of us," this, in fact, means you are no longer a member of society.

Mafia state language is irrational, it appeals to emotions, not to reason

Everyone who speaks for the regime speaks that language. It is irrational and not open to discussion; it appeals to emotions and not to reason. It is a language of a monologue and not dialogue; it is a language of declarations; it dictates instead of discussing or relating. Speakers using such language often use phrases that dehumanize an opponent or they affix derogatory labels while ascribing universal human values and justice exclusively to themselves. Typical examples of such language are Dmitry Medvedev's posts in Telegram.

The post-Soviet mafia state's language uses the Soviet propaganda lexicon familiar to many people and still not forgotten. This takes people mentally back to the Soviet Union and its familiar world view of a standoff between "two systems." In 2022-2023, officials peppered their speeches with words and phrases such as "puppets," "henchmen," "masters of the world," "plotting," "pumping resources," "a system of hoodwinking the masses," "system of global exploitation," etc.

Sanctifying power

In a mafia state with imperial ambitions, the regime starts to acquire sacred meaning. Those in power believe their power was granted by God, and they try to impose this view on society as a whole. Around the mid-2000s, Vladimir Putin apparently believed he was chosen and has a mission to save Russia. Not only did he start perceiving himself as Savior of Russia but also the propaganda machine started building this image as well. Putin's numerous trips to Athos were intended to project the perception of Putin as having been inspired by divine power.

Accidentally finding himself in the seat of power, the head of the mafia state gradually starts believing in his chosenness and purposefulness, and also starts realizing it's impossible to give up power.

Whereas in a democratic state, a government's legitimacy is confirmed by elections, in a mafia state it is God who confirms it. In fact, God is written into the secular state's Constitution and mentioned in the national anthem.

The sanctification of power leads to fighting viciously those who try to contest it, by seeking to invoke not secular, but mystical forces in this fight, even if the attempts to contest power seem insignificant from the outside. The Shaman of Yakutia, Gabyshev, who walked to Moscow on foot in order to "banish Putin," gathering supporters and believers on the way, was placed in a psychiatric hospital for forced treatment.

Also indicative is the disproportionately harsh sentence imposed on participants of the "punk prayer" at the Cathedral of Christ the Savior, who begged Virgin Mary: "Mother of God, banish Putin!" Pussy Riot members received actual prison terms.

Schema-hegumen [a high degree of monasticism in the Orthodox Church] Sergei was also treated harshly: he was expelled from the church and sentenced to 3.5 years in prison for a number of crimes, although clearly, he was persecuted primarily for trying to contest Vladimir Putin's right to run Russia, and for calling on Putin to repent.

The role of religion in the mafia state

A mafia state top brass' religiousness is totally pragmatic. A mafia state thus differs from states like Iran, where religion dictates the rules of life. In a mafia state, religion serves the ruling group's interests. Patriarchal religiousness imbues society with a *feeling of submission and the perception that all that happens are trials from God that one must endure without grumbling.* Faith is irrational; appealing to religious postulates makes it possible to go beyond the bounds of rational critique, to turn it off. Religion presents society with a specific model, a specific framework within which an person has to exist; in the circumstances, the person can give up the fight and individuality because, by following customs, and adopting the proper habits, the person can lead an irreproachable life without much effort. This applies to the entire model of a patriarchal society based on traditions. In a mafia state, the priority thus is clear: faith is needed in order to implement the regime's objectives.

During the post-Soviet years, the Russian Eastern Orthodox Church, and Eastern Orthodoxy itself essentially underwent a serious mutation, becoming an ideological servant of the mafia state. The Russian Orthodox Church became an important element in formulating state policy and its mythology.

The ideological merging of church and state was on full display during Russia's military actions in Ukraine.

In contrast to the Catholic Pope, who called for just one thing: "In God's name, I beg you, stop this slaughter!", Patriarch Kirill contended that the war is against Russia: "Many rise against Rus,[229] and many people's heads are spinning with the desire to destroy Rus, its distinct identity, its independence, its freedom. And, therefore, today we must especially reinforce our faith, fill our cathedrals, pray for the authorities and the military, for our families and dear ones, pray for the Orthodox Church, which preserves Holy Rus's spiritual unity in these most difficult conditions."

The Eastern Orthodox traditions, rituals, church services, and the Patriarch's statements – all essentially became just a righteous wrapper for Russia's neo-imperialist ideology.

229 The patriarch deliberately uses the appellation referring to Russia as a Slavic, historic, and sacred entity.

Derationalizing the thinking process and searching for a "youth serum"

A loyal companion to religious derationalized thinking is the spread of various beliefs, including non-traditional medicine, various magic substances, and miracles as such. It goes beyond mere faith – authorities actually start investing state funds, and supporting these "miracle cures" on an official level.

One of the first high-profile cases in this series was "Petrik-gate" – a scientific scandal around entrepreneur Viktor Petrik's projects in 2009. At the time, with the support of State Duma chairman and United Russia Party's Supreme Council's head Boris Gryzlov, Viktor Petrik lobbied to have his water purification filters used in all state and municipal facilities all over Russia. The plan was to spend 15 trillion rubles in federal funds in order to install the filters as part of the party's "Clean Water" program (in place since 2006); the program was to be completed by 2020. A scandal raged around Petrik's designs, however, which, ultimately, were declared unscientific.

The inevitable aging of Russian authorities leads them to seek ways to extend their life and fortify their health; hence, aside from striving to have the latest modern medicine at their service, they turn toward non-traditional medicine.

One of the latest fads among the Russian ruling group is the faith in magical properties of a musk deer's preputial gland secretions (musk). Musk deer is a small saber-toothed deer. Musk is an odorous substance that forms in a small pouch on the male's belly. Using this scent, male deer attract females. A male musk deer produces at most 20 grams of musk per year. Musk is considered a treatment for all ailments. It is ground into a powder or distilled. It is believed to help with oncological diseases of any type, male and female infertility, epilepsy, psychological illnesses, and is also thought to have rejuvenating and body-strengthening properties.

In 2016, the faith in musk's magical properties was confirmed financially when Vladimir Putin allocated 1.522 billion rubles in federal funds to set up a nursery for musk deer in Altai's *Belukha* nature park.[230] The official basis was "to provide Russian Federation athletic teams and its special contingent, which currently numbers over 20,000 people, with innovative pharmacological substances that increase the level of physical fitness and possess preventative and therapeutic properties for a number of illnesses." Evidently, however, it was not intended for athletes but for members of the elite. Not surprisingly, part of the allocated 1.522 billion disappeared, while the project itself was not implemented as originally planned.[231]

---

230 https://gxpnews.net/2016/07/v-rossii-budut-razrabatyvat-innovacionnye-preparaty-na-osnove-muskusa-kabargi/ [in Russian].

231 https://istories.media/investigations/2020/06/11/olenerazvodi/ [in Russian].

Other Russian officials swear by the curative effects of velvet antler baths using Altai wapiti (a large deer) antlers. Extracts from such antlers are ascribed medicinal properties in folk medicine, but there is no scientific proof. Moreover, the animals are subjected to horrible suffering: they are tied down or viced in and lifted so they helplessly dangle, and the still-tender, not yet ossified antlers are cut off, often with a plain saw.

The *Proekt* (Project) publication noted in its research[232] that Defense Minister Sergei Shoigu was among the first people interested in velvet antler baths; he then recommended them to Vladimir Putin, who tried them and liked them. After Putin, the baths became popular among the Russian elite.

---

232 https://www.proekt.media/investigation/chem-boleet-putin/#top_doctors [in Russian].

Revising history

In 2018, the authors of "Russia Against History. Punishment for Revision" noted: "History is becoming a dangerous science." The report was prepared by Agora International Human Rights Group and included information on monitoring 100 separate instances, including criminal prosecutions and administrative action in which Russian authorities concealed archival documents, applied a restrictive regulation, and, in the most widespread form of interference, barred informational materials under the guise of fighting extremism.

The "riskiest" topics that Agora identified in its report are WWII and the USSR's role in it. Agora experts noted that sanctification of the Soviet Union's victory in The Great Patriotic War (WWII), punishment for "insulting" and "desecrating" commemorative dates and symbols, restricting interpretations of historical events or personalities to those in line with the official interpretation; prohibiting academic works; labeling archival documents as "extremist materials," and persecuting historians in general falls in line with the overarching recent trend by Russian authorities to restrict freedom of speech.

During *perestroika*, it was natural to abandon a unified historical doctrine, and the collapse of the USSR was accompanied by a rejection of Marxist-Leninist concepts of the historical process and of a class-based approach to describing historical events. The building of a new authoritarian regime, however, renewed the need for a unitary approach to history.

The state started making its first systemic attempts to control the cultural space under the guise of defending history during Dmitry Medvedev's presidency. In 2009, Medvedev issued a special decree establishing a "Commission to counter the attempts to falsify history to the detriment of Russia's interests." In 2012, Vladimir Putin signed a Decree to recreate the Russian Military-Historical Society in order to counteract attempts to distort history. It was announced that important objectives were "defending historical truth, our people's heroic exploit in defending the Fatherland," counteracting "historic revisionism" with its attempts to "equate the USSR to Nazi Germany and to place responsibility on the USSR (and, essentially, Russia as successor of the Soviet Union) for WWII." This was triggered by an ideological battle between historians and propagandists regarding several historical events that include:

- The "Katyn affair"[233]
- The Molotov-Ribbentrop Pact, Soviet cooperation with Germany and plans to divide Poland
- The exploit of "Panfilov's 28 men" near Dubosekovo Junction.[234]

---

233 Katyn – site of the massacre of 22,000 Polish officers and prisoners of war in World War II in spring 1940. Claiming that the Nazis had implemented the killings, the USSR denied responsibility until 1990, when it acknowledged that the NKVD had carried out the massacre.

234 Supposed heroic resistance of 28 members of Red Army Infantry in November 1941 that stopped German tank and infantry advance on Moscow. Subject of a popular Russian movie *Panfilov's 28 Men*.

In 2014, a special provision was added to the Criminal Code with liability for rehabilitating Nazism. This article started being applied in instances of clearly offensive statements with the use of Third Reich symbolism but also in instances of ordinary discussions regarding the USSR's role during WWII and reminders that Stalin's USSR closely collaborated with Hitler's Germany. No one was convicted under this article in 2014, but in 2017, eight people were convicted. In 2021, this article was expanded to include criminal liability for disseminating false information regarding WWII veterans, defaming the memory of the Fatherland's defenders, or debasing WWII veterans' honor and dignity.

In 2022, Vladimir Putin thus summarized the state's work "defending history": "It is known that if someone wants to deprive a state of sovereignty and turn its citizens into vassals, they start precisely with rewriting this country's history, in order to deprive people of their roots, condemn them to oblivion. <...> Such attempts have been made regarding Russia, too, and they are not stopping, but we established a firm defense against them in a timely manner."[235]

Rewriting history applies not only to past wars; it touches the present, too. In spring 2022, after Russian forces invaded Ukraine, criminal liability was introduced in Russia, punishable by up to 15 years in prison,

---

235 https://historyrussia.org/sobytiya/vystuplenie-prezidenta-na-vstreche-s-istorikami-i-predstavitelyami-traditsionnykh-religij.html [in Russian].

for disseminating "fakes" about the military operation, appealing for sanctions, and discrediting the Russian armed forces.

Another repercussion of twentieth century history that became so painful for twenty-first century Russia and determined Russia's present under Vladimir Putin are the activities of the NKVD (People's Commissariat for Internal Affairs) and KGB in general and the repressions of the Great Terror in particular. For example, on March 12, 2014, the Inter-agency Commission on Protecting State Secrets adopted Decision No. 2-C "To extend the time limit for the classification of sealed information constituting a state secret that was classified by the *Cheka* and KGB from1917-1991." By this decision, many Soviet state security agencies' documents will remain classified until the year 2044. As a result, materials involving, for example, mass repressions, remain inaccessible not only to researchers but also to victims' families.

Post-Soviet Russian society insufficiently deliberated the attitude toward repressions, the Great Terror period, and Joseph Stalin, which may have become a building block in the foundation of the new round of authoritarianism in Russia.

Stalinism's most distinguishing feature, its lineal trait (which arose from the beginning of the Bolshevik rule and did not disappear after Stalin died) is the concept of terror as a universal tool for solving any political or social issue – this was noted by [the late] historian and *Memorial* international society chairman of the board Arseny Roginsky during his December 2008 speech at an international conference on Stalinist history:[236] "In modern Russia, the authorities have always experienced a deficit of legitimacy. At the same time, after the collapse of the USSR, the population experienced a deficit of identity. Both the authorities and the population sought ways to make up for these deficits with the image of a Great Russia, whose successor is today's Russia. Images of the "bright past" proposed by the authorities in the 1990s (Petr Stolypin, Peter the Great, etc.), were not embraced: they derived from a too distant past and had too little connection to the present. Gradually and subconsciously, the concept of Great Russia was grafted onto the Soviet period, in particular, the Stalinist era," – Roginsky noted. "An image of a happy and glorious past was needed in order to consolidate the population, reinstate the indisputability of the regime's authority, strengthen the regime's hierarchy, etc. Regardless of these intentions, against the backdrop of a panorama of a great power rising anew, still 'encircled by enemies,' the mustached profile of the great leader is coming through again. This was unavoidable and logical."

In 2017, almost 10 years after Roginsky's speech, Vladimir Putin told the film director Oliver Stone in an interview that "excessive demonization of Stalin is one of the ways, one of the methods of attacking the Soviet Union and Russia."

---

236 http://www.intelros.ru/pdf/60_paralel/36/04.pdf [in Russian].

In lieu of conclusion

While this book was being written, the situation in Russia became even more definitive. Even fewer players now have direct contact with Putin and manipulate him: merely a few people, the most trusted individuals who can negotiate on behalf of the mafia state and have the freedom to make decisions about resources on the scale of the state budget. All of them, together with Putin, strive toward the obvious goals – increasing their wealth and retaining their power.

In pursuit of this goal, they direct and define Russia's path in order to make the world bipolar, with Russia as China's junior partner and ally counteracting the U.S. and U.S. allies.

A recent key event in Putin's Russia was the elimination of another significant player – the assassination of Yevgeny Prigozhin, which can be considered a perfect example of how a mafia state operates. These actions are in line with gangster logic. The mafia state initially nurtured a powerful unofficial figure; when he threatened the power of the head of the clan, they did away with him in cold blood without turning to any official institutions of a normal state, such as courts, prosecution, investigation, etc.

Prigozhin's case showed the world once and for all that we are not dealing with a state. The mafia state model that formed in Russia only looks like a state externally and is successfully camouflaged as such, deceiving everyone. In fact, however, the government has long been forced out by a criminal hierarchy that seeks to expand its influence far beyond Russia. Dealing with this is not easy, but imperative.

www.ingramcontent.com/pod-product-compliance
Lightning Source LLC
LaVergne TN
LVHW021717190325
806372LV00004B/47
* 9 7 8 9 6 5 5 7 5 4 1 4 8 *